THE OTHER WAY AROUND

THE TOWA TRILOGY
BOOK ONE

NOON WESTBROOK

NEXUS PARTNERS, LLC.

ACKNOWLEDGMENTS

I would like to thank my family for their unwavering support, encouragement, and valuable guidance in shaping the trajectory of my project. I could not have completed this journey without you.

I am grateful to the amazing artists who participated in the *TOWA Cover Competition*. Your unique talents, skills, and creativity, have left an indelible mark on the visual embodiment of the book cover. Each of you are awesome and uniquely gifted. I wish you the best on future projects.

I would like to thank my diligent proofreaders, layout team, and print support for the role they played in ensuring the project was completed with care.

Lastly, thank you to everyone who played a part in equipping me with the necessary resources and partnership to complete my first novel. From art direction to web design, marketing, and printing, your generous contributions have not gone unnoticed or under-appreciated.

I humbly extend a big hug and thank everyone who helped me get this story out of my heart and into these pages.

Sincerely,
Noon Westbrook

CHAPTER 1

*A*nother day, another hectic lunch rush. I was in the car trying to decide if I wanted to grab a bite to eat. "But, the wait times in these drive-throughs are so damn long this time of day. And honestly, I should go to the grocery store. Healthy choices, Naomi," I said to myself.

Before I could respond and talk myself into a poor dietary choice, my cell phone started vibrating from inside my purse. I smiled at the timing. I was pretty sure it was Kinney calling me from the airport. He and the kids were going to visit his dad in Belize. In the past, we tried to visit at least once a year. But we hadn't been back for a few years with the kids being in so many activities (literally soccer, football, basketball, and dance) and Kinney trying to make moves and climb the corporate ladder.

Most people here in Middleton would have considered a summer in Belize to be a fantasy getaway, and they would not be wrong. But I was so looking forward to a few days alone! If it hadn't been for a keynote speech I committed to deliver back in the fall, I would have been passing through airport security with them. "In due time, but right now, I need to bask in the joy of my solitude." I motioned my thumb to the call button on my

1

steering wheel. I pressed the button and noticed "Valley Spring Regional Hospital" across my car's dashboard. "Who in the world would be calling me from the hospital? It has to be the wrong number." By that point, I'd already answered.

I uttered a polite but hesitant hello. A woman's voice responded. "Hi, my name is Barbara Dobbs, and I'm calling from Valley Spring Regional. Am I speaking with Naomi Martinez?" In that instant, I thought, "Well, that's bizarre - to my knowledge, no one I know is in the hospital. And Valley Spring is quite a ways from us." My mind started racing, and I instantly began to worry. "Did something happen to Kinney and the kids on the way to the airport?" That's the only possible explanation, and now lunch is the furthest thing from my mind. Puzzlement and panic are evident in my response. "Yes, this is Naomi. Oh my God, has there been an accident?! Are my husband and kids okay?" Barbara responded, "Um, I'm not sure, Mrs. Martinez. I'm so sorry to have startled you! I'm a case manager here at Valley Spring Regional Hospital. I was given your name and number as an emergency contact..."

Before she could finish her statement, I interrupted, "By who?!?" Given my initial alarm and confusion, Barbara's tone also began to sound puzzled. "We have a patient here who directed us to contact you in the event of a medical emergency. Her name is Loretta Wade. She indicated that..."

I interrupted her yet again, "Wait, I'm sorry. Who?!?" She repeated the unfamiliar name, emphasizing each syllable as if English might not be my first language.

"No. I'm sorry, dear. I don't know anyone by that name," I replied with certainty.

There was an awkward silence on the line before Barbara responded apologetically, "I just keep apologizing, but I have you, Naomi Martinez, listed as an emergency contact with this phone number for Loretta Wade. But you do not know who she is." I could sense how perplexed she was, and at this point, I was racking my brain and thumbing through my mental files. It isn't one of my relatives. I've never had any patients by that name, and I still recall the names of patients I saw back when my clinic was open. Kinney doesn't have anyone named Loretta on his side of the family (at least that I know of). "Could it be someone from high school?" I wondered. In three seconds, I had exhausted all the possibilities that came to mind.

"Barbara, I wish I could be more helpful here, but I have another call to jump to. I hope you find the Naomi you're looking for." She apologized yet again, thanked me for my time, and I hung up.

I couldn't get over how certain she was that I was a stranger's emergency contact. Then, I thought this wouldn't be the first time I was mistaken for another Naomi. There were many of 'us' on the internet—all shades, races, sizes and genders too. When I was in college, there were two of us. Back then, I thought, "Another Naomi O'Hara…at the same college? What are the odds?" Our paths never crossed in person. Had it not been for an errant hold on my account, I still wouldn't have known of my namesake's existence.

I went to the cashier's office to dispute the incorrectly assigned bill that held up my registration. The exchange with the cashier wasn't pleasant. I'll never forget his smugness on the other side of the plexiglass. Or how it took 25 minutes and two other cashiers to solve the mystery of my identity, begrudgingly acknowledge their mistake, and then correct it. The best part was their nerve—to act like they did me a favor by correcting their clerical errors.

I remember him saying, "In the future, you may want to use a middle initial or something to distinguish yourself better. It would help you avoid situations like this." My 19-year-old self replied, "The fact that I don't have a middle name is distinguishing enough. You all might pay closer attention to detail in the future."

I recall that moment fondly because it was the first time that 'grin and bear it' Naomi took second stage to who I would have to become. Reflecting on my upbringing, I realize how 'demure' I was. I spent most of my childhood as a non-confrontational girl. I wasn't particularly congenial, well-developed physically, or athletic. I was more... bookish. I excelled academically (graduating near the top of my class). I never had any behavior or disciplinary issues (at school or home). I played flute and clarinet in the band (concert and symphonic). And I didn't socialize much outside of my closest friends.

In college, I blossomed socially, expanded my circle, and became active on campus through student government. But that day in the cashier's office was an important display of power—it was a power I always had inside of me. Sure, I stood up for myself, but I did so in a professional, direct, and unexpected way. I would have to tap into this muscle memory regularly to overcome people in positions to undermine, gaslight, demean, or thwart me because of my gender, ethnicity, skin tone, or name. Subtle racism pulses through the air here in Middleton, and my radar is well-attuned when directed at me or my family.

The mystery phone call from the hospital helped me decide on lunch. It had me so distracted that I didn't even remember parking the car in front of the grocery store. I gathered myself to go inside and purchase a few items for my days at home alone. I reached for my purse and glasses on the passenger seat and entered the store. I grabbed a basket and began gathering—a bundle of celery, a green pepper, and a bag of premade salad. Before I could get to the meat section for a few lean proteins, my purse started vibrating again. The screen read "Valley Spring Regional Hospital." "Seriously?" I thought. My first instinct was to ignore it, given our recent conversation. But I suppose curiosity had gotten the better of me.

CHAPTER 2

*I*t's been a few weeks since the kid's last day of school. Sleeping in has been a real treat for them and one less daily tribulation for me. With school being out for the summer, I'm sure other children besides mine are waking up with smiles on their faces after sleeping in, and parents are waking up irritable at the thought of three long months at home with their children. As parents, we all love our children, but I'm not ashamed to say I need a break sometimes. That said, our house had a different energy this morning.

"All right, gang. Let's get it moving!" Kinney bellowed from the upstairs foyer, echoing through the hall and bedrooms. I was helping our youngest, Kinsey, get her most crucial travel items packed up, which included two books, 24 crayons, a notepad for doodling, a stuffed rabbit named Dusty, and a hand-me-down iPad she won from her brothers.

She hollered back with a twinge of annoyance in her melodic voice, "We're almost ready, Dad! Be patient!" I cracked a bit of a smile, but you must watch out for Kinsey. At four years old, she was the most precocious of our three kids. She'd been verbal since she was six months old and always had some-

5

thing to say about something at home. Honestly, she'd taken me by surprise with some of the things that came out of that little mouth of hers. Sure, it had gotten her into some trouble now and then, but she was learning early that it wasn't always what you say, but how and when you say it that makes the difference.

Down the hall, the twins are making sure that each has packed the shoes and outfits that the other will want to wear while they are gone. "Dude, why wouldn't you take the blue Vans to go with that?!" Noel asked disapprovingly.

Irritated, Nick replied, "Because you are not wearing these and getting sand in them like you did my Jordans!" Noel, the older of the identical pair by seven minutes, responded with a shoulder shrug and head shake, prompting Nick to give in and pack the shoes anyway. Nicholas and Noland are night and day in personality despite being virtually identical in looks.

Noland, or Noel as everyone calls him, is Mr. Personality. He's one of those people who have the 'it' factor, which can be a double-edged sword. His classmates love him, especially the girls. He does things well without even trying, which his baseball and basketball coaches mistake for lack of effort. Knowing how often teachers and coaches misunderstand our children, Kinney and I watch for 'authority figures' giving him a harder time because of his swag. We know a future homecoming king is inside this socially adept, style-savvy ten-year-old.

Nicholas (or Nick for short) is the quintessential 'strong-but-silent' type. Where Noel is thin and long-limbed, Nick is a bit shorter and a bit heartier around the midsection. But it's all muscle. He loves contact sports like wrestling, rugby, and football. When he plays at our athletic club or nearby parks, he always plays with the older kids and holds his own. Like his brother, he was also a great student, but social interaction outside of sports, home, and family wasn't his cup of tea. Nick was about as easygoing a kid as there is, except for picking up after himself. I was more likely to find an old candy wrapper under his bed than a missing assignment.

Nick and Noel were yin and yang—night and day, but we loved their bond as twins. For a moment, I worried how they would embrace a younger sibling, but they immediately put my concerns to rest. They have been loving and protective big brothers to their little sister, and together, they are my everything.

Kinney made his way down the hall, and our eyes locked. I shifted my eyes toward Kinsey, who packed headphones, lip balm, and gummy bears into her backpack. "She's so official," he laughs. We kissed, and I passed him to check in with the boys.

"Alright, guys. If you pack less, you can come home with more stuff," Kinney reminds them. Nick and Noel looked at each other and looked down at their suitcases with strategic concern. I smiled and said, "Don't worry, we can borrow a suitcase or two from your grandpa if needed."

Yes!" whispered Noel while Nick analyzed and concluded, "Smart idea, Mom."

"Kinsey's already ready, so y'all better get these bags down to the car before she and Dad leave y'all here!" I joked. While the boys gathered the final essentials into their backpacks, I went downstairs and headed toward the garage. Kinney had just loaded his suitcase into the back of his SUV.

"Pops ain't nearly ready for these monsters," Kinney said.

"Oh, I'm sure he is, and I'm ready for them to be gone!" I motioned as if I was shooing them out of the house. Kinney looked at me with a playful frown and said, "You can't wait for us to get outta here!"

"Oh, poor Kinney has to take the kids to Belize," I said sarcastically. Kinney smiled and laughed deeply. "So, no wild parties while we're gone, Lil Nay-Nay." I replied, "Who me?" while showing off a few of my dance moves from days long past. He imitated his father's Belizean patois and said flirtingly,

"Aarite, weh gaan ahn gyal," coming closer and moving rhythmically with me.

"Don't get me wrong. I'm looking forward to seeing Dad after so long, but I'm looking forward to seeing you on the beach in a two-piece."

"Yeah, I bet you are!" I replied. "'Mom Bod Meets Dad Bod on Belizean Beach'—I can see the headline now!" We laughed and hugged a while longer as the sound of children dragging luggage towards us grew louder.

* * *

PEOPLE WHO HEAR my name often look surprised when they first see me or see us as a family. With a last name like Martinez, they seemingly expect a less melanated family to appear in front of them. When we show up at the kids' events, business parties, or other social engagements and they see my beautiful, brown-skinned family, it's like their minds can't comprehend these Black people having a presumably Spanish last name.

My maiden name is O'Hara, taken from my Creole father. He was a fairer-skinned man with stunning, greenish-gray eyes. I remember him being so bashful about them growing up, but he wasn't shy about having a good time with his boys performing at the nightclub.

Meanwhile, my mother was a Black woman whose family came from the East Coast, as far as I knew. Compared to my Dad, with his light skin and green eyes, she was considerably less 'exotic' by colorist standards. Despite growing up in the era she did, her mocha skin didn't stop her from a successful career as a nurse.

Martinez is Kinney's paternal family surname. His father is Afro-Amerindian, descended from the children of West African and Native American people. His father's earliest ancestors migrated from the Deep South through Louisiana and sailed

8

across the Gulf of Mexico to the Yucatan, where they could live freely and grow their family. So even though Kinney's dad was born in the United States, he inherited the Martinez family estate and several acres of land in Belize. He's been down there for more than three decades. He's always enjoyed our visits 'home,' but even more so as our family has grown.

Kinney is the regional sales lead for a major software company and does very well. For most of his climb up the corporate ladder, I had a psychiatric practice and taught classes remotely at various colleges and universities. They say behind every great man is a great woman. Well, this great woman was in front—managing career, motherhood, and wisdom with grace and style.

Kinney and I met in our early twenties during our senior year in college. And, like me, he swore never to return to Middleton after graduation. His first job took him to the West Coast, where I completed my Ph.D. and started practicing. We both grew in our careers but were ready to start a family together. Three kids and twenty years later, here we are. I made the sacrifice of closing my practice to focus on the family, and our move to Middleton allowed us to be closer to 'home.' The demands of Kinney's job and travel schedule, combined with the twin's increasing activities, forced my hand a bit, but I made the decision to stay home and keep things afloat. I'd be lying if I said I didn't miss the hustle and flow of seeing patients and lecturing students some days. But my children needed me to be present, and I would regret not being there for them and all their moments. Good or bad. Happy or sad.

Other than that, it's pretty simple—people don't associate our Spanish-Latin surname with such an unapologetically Black family. When you add that we've afforded ourselves a very comfortable, plentiful lifestyle, we trigger more questions than answers for the simple-minded, middle-class American folks here in Middleton. And we love it.

* * *

THE SOUND of excited chatter and rolling luggage filled the space from the kitchen to the garage. Kinney and I looked down at the traveling trio of Noel, Nick, and Kinsey. Noel, like the team spokesperson he is, announces, "Okay, Mom, we have everything we need until you get down there." I bent down and said, "I bet you do, but let's make sure." I playfully quizzed each of the kids on the contents of their backpacks while Kinney loaded their luggage. I thought, "I cherish these little monsters, but there is a part of me that will enjoy not having to take care of anyone but myself for the next week or so."

I told them, "There's one last thing you need before you go... breakfast." The kids enthusiastically went to the other side of the kitchen to find bacon, eggs, and their favorite cereals ready for pouring.

As parents, we can become consumed by work and our kids' activities. Add to that an array of other duties and distractions that take up the remaining space in our days and nights. By the end of a day, week, month, or whatever, we're not left with sufficient energy or time to care for or tend to ourselves. I should know—I wrote a book on the subject and had a series of consultation calls to start once Kinney and the kids left. As much as I would miss them, I thought, "My time will come, and I shouldn't feel guilty about it. I need to embrace and enjoy it."

I watched Kinney and the kids enjoy the breakfast I prepared while cleaning up a bit. After a final round of hugs, tickles, and kisses, they all piled into the SUV. A forty-five-minute drive to the airport for a midday departure to Belize. Without me.

When the garage door closed, I took a deep breath and braced myself for some much-deserved 'me-time.'

CHAPTER 3

*W*ith Kinney and the kids gone, it's just me, myself, and I at home alone. "What is this?" I asked myself. "This must be silence. Hello, Silence, my old friend..." I hummed the rest of the melody from the classic song as I made my way from the garage to the kitchen. On this day, 'me-time' began with a nice cup of coffee.

Some people have their comfort foods. Well, I have comfort coffee. I don't drink it just to wake up or to get that mid-afternoon energy boost so many people need. I love the taste of it, and while I have standard fare blends for every day, today was special. And a special day called for my top-shelf beans. I debated between my beloved Hawaiian Kona Peaberry and my ultra-rare Kopi Luwak. While the taste of the Kopi is akin to a sensual, out-of-body experience, there's a dreamy, tranquilizing vibe to the Kona that just fit my moment to a tee.

With coffee brewed and tablet in hand, I plopped onto the couch, draped in my most plush robe. I opened my tablet to access my email inbox and calendar. Rather than see patients or teach courses, I consult family law attorneys, therapists, department chairs, and others with some interest in self-care therapies for victims of trauma and abuse.

Before I closed my private practice a few years back, I made a bet on the idea of a self-care regimen for people who had suffered and survived life-altering traumas, both physical and emotional. I published a series of papers covering eight dimensions of wellness. After some success on the lecture circuit, I developed those data and research findings into a therapeutic behavioral model for self-care and emotional healing. The improvement in my patient's quality of life and testimonials were proof of my model's effectiveness, and I was able to merchandise that successfully across care facilities and mental health services nationwide.

My calendar was lighter than usual, adding to my relaxation after that first luxurious sip of Kona. I usually have about eight practice consultations a week and take on two or three larger speaking events a month, like the one I had coming up later that week. "Unpacking the Evolution of Self-care with Dr. Naomi Martinez" at my alma mater. That's the only real reason I didn't leave with Kinney and the kids, but this Zen moment is everything. I tapped on my first consult session of the day. "Dr. Riann? Hi, it's Dr. Martinez. How are you?... I'm happy to hear that. Let's catch up a bit on the Wilson case."

* * *

I LOVE (or loved) my job. Honestly, I would rather be working than dealing with some of the pedestrian hassles that occur with my family on an average day in Middleton. A great example was three or four days before the kids' last day of school. I received a frantic call from one of the teachers at Kinsey's school. Before I get into this story, I should say that I have deep respect and appreciation for those inclined to give their heart and energy as educators. Given everything they endure from other people's kids, there's not enough money to reward them. But some of these folks are way too much. Kinsey's preschool teacher, Mrs. Wofford, was a prime example.

"Mrs. Martinez, we've had a behavior issue with Kinsey that I think would be best discussed in person." Knowing Kinsey's special mouth, I wasn't alarmed per se, but her tone was both hurt and anxious.

"I'll be there right away. Where is Kinsey now?"

"She's right here with Father Kemp and I."

"Oh, okay. Please let her know I'll be right there."

Kinsey attends a Catholic preschool, but we are not Catholics. Despite very Christian upbringings, we'd consider ourselves spiritual and probably balk at being labeled 'religious.' Anyway, Kinsey walked from her pew with the rest of her classmates during afternoon mass to receive communion. Now, in her four-year-old mind, that wasn't the body and blood of Christ. That was a delicious vanilla wafer cookie and scrumptious Welch's Grape Drink. Not juice. Drink.

Kinsey, being a non-Catholic student in a Catholic school, should have stood and approached Father Kemp with her hands crossed over her chest in the form of an X (to publicly identify that not only is she the class's only Black girl, but also the only Black, non- Catholic girl in Pre-K). Well, apparently, Kinsey was going to have juice and cookies on this particular day. When it was her turn to approach the priest, she extended her hand. Father Kemp smiled, and she partook in the sacrament. Seeing Kinsey return toward her pew chewing must have sent Mrs. Wofford off the deep end. Hence, her hysterical call and my visit to the school. "Supermom to the rescue, yet again," I sighed as I pulled into her school's driveway.

I signed in, and the receptionist greeted me with a half smile, to which I returned an equally false grin. Father Kemp and Kinsey saw me first, and we both smiled. Kinsey got up and ran over to hug my leg. Father Kemp said, "Thanks for coming over on such short notice." A loud sniffle came from the other side of the office. An emotional Mrs. Wofford sat with a tissue near her eye, dabbing invisible tears.

I masked my amusement with a false look of concern. "So, what happened here?" I asked. Mrs. Wofford replayed her account of the afternoon's traumatic event at the hands of my four-year-old daughter. The way this woman carried on about Kinsey receiving communion, you would have thought Jesus Christ himself showed up in person. All I could think was, "Woman, I know you're not this serious?" I'm pretty sure I smirked a little bit. Father Kemp wasn't making matters any better as he blushed with embarrassment from her spiritual meltdown. I found it hilarious because I know how much Kinsey loves cookies. Considering that she'd gone to mass after mass and never done that, she ought to be commended. In a way, I was comforted by my little brainiac of a daughter behaving like any other kid would. "If you put cookies and juice in their face enough times, eventually, they will take them," I thought. Looking down at her, she became more confused by Mrs. Wofford's response and started to tremble. Tears would follow, so I cut the rest of the teacher's emotional sideshow short.

"I get that she was not supposed to accept communion in your eyes. But I take offense at how you keep reiterating that Kinsey isn't Catholic, as though Catholics are the only religion that takes communion. She doesn't even have to be Christian to partake, but she did, and here we all are. No fire, no brimstone. I guess that means God has bigger things on his plate. Maybe you should as well." A look of shock came over the teacher's face and a glimpse of approval over Kinsey's. We left the school, went home, and promptly baked a batch of cookies just for us.

It's times like that when a part of me regrets being so 'available.' Not long ago, my overbooked patient schedule, speaking events, and course calendar would have rendered an episode like that impossible. But then again, I wouldn't want to miss an opportunity like that. To teach this overly religiously preoccupied teacher a lesson about the history of communion beyond Catholicism in front of my only daughter.

All in all, such are the blessings and curses of living in a place like Middleton. While Kinsey is one of the very few non-white students at her school, there are no teachers of color on the staff currently. Like the Lord, unconscious bias can work in mysterious ways, especially when teaching, grading, and interacting with children of color. While I may have been annoyed with the whole situation, it gave me yet another opportunity to show Kinsey the kind of woman I expected her to become.

More often than not, I viewed being 'available' as me doing God's work. And to that, I'd say, "Amen."

* * *

THE REST of the morning was smooth sailing, and my afternoon was free. I thought, "I'm not sure what I'm going to do with myself, but I should probably stop by Berkshire Square and look around for the two-piece bikini Kinney mentioned."

And I was getting hungry. "I'm really about to take care of myself today!" I closed my tablet and went upstairs to get myself together for a much-deserved day off. As I neared the multi-acre, high-end shopping complex Berkshire Square, I was floored by the number of people out and about. I looked at the time and thought, "Another day, another hectic lunch rush..."

CHAPTER 4

$\mathcal{I}$ answered the phone this time, and a different voice greeted me on the other end. "Mrs. Martinez, I'm Mary Litzen. Thanks for picking up. I know you spoke to another case manager a moment ago..." "Yes, about Loretta Wade..." I replied, feeling a little uneasy.

"Yes, exactly. Ms. Wade is unconscious. While I cannot disclose full details with you over the phone, her condition is dire, and well, we're not sure how much time we have left."

As I racked my brain to make the association, I wondered why in the world a social worker would be calling me.

"That's right. I did, and as I told her, that name isn't ringing any bells," I replied, trying to hide my annoyance.

"Yes," Mary said. "We understand, but I just wanted to double-check and do my due diligence."

I replied, "I'm sorry that I can't be of more help." I thought to myself, the only person I can think of is a woman I recently met, but her name is Dixie. And I don't even know her last name. Out loud, I asked, "Mary, the woman...Loretta. Does she go by the name Dixie by chance?"

"Dixie?" Mary asked. "I'm not sure, but I can check on that

and see what I can find out." Barbara interrupted and responded to Mary, "Loretta had a visitor here earlier—her sister, I believe. I'll go see if she's still here and ask her." Mary asked me to hold on for just a minute.

While I was still on the line, Barbara returned to Mary's office. "Hi, Naomi, this is Barbara. Loretta's sister is here, and she confirmed that Loretta does go by the nickname Dixie, but no one in the family calls her that."

"Dixie?!? She can't be serious," I thought. At this point, I was standing in the middle of the grocery store aisle. In shock and disbelief, I left my basket of groceries in the middle of the aisle and started walking back toward my car. I gathered my composure and continued speaking to the social workers.

"Okay, I want to make sure that I'm hearing you correctly. Loretta Wade is Dixie? You must pardon my surprise, but I don't have a 'relationship' with her. I only met her a week or so ago."

"I see...well Loretta, ahem, Dixie put your name down as her emergency contact," she said.

The words fell out of my mouth, "Now, why would she do that!?"

I was stunned. "I don't know her like that. I met her recently, and when I say recently, I mean one conversation a couple of weeks ago at best." The social worker sounded just as confused as I was.

"So, you and Loretta aren't related, aren't friends per se, and only recently met? Well, she has your name down, and when we couldn't confirm who you were, we had to notify Child Services. They should be here soon. If you do not want to take her son, we can let him go with them," she said.

Feeling bombarded with all this, my emotions were clear in my voice. "Wait, what?!? Her son?" I repeated with agitation. "What do you mean if I don't want to take her son? Take him where?"

I only realized who these social workers were talking about two minutes ago. Twenty minutes ago, I thought my family had been in an accident, and now I'm sitting in my car asking myself, "What the hell is going on?" This must be some mistake. Surely, this woman wouldn't leave her son in my care without so much as a conversation. But then again, I don't know what is going through her mind, and she's not conscious enough to explain herself.

I asked the social worker, "What exactly is happening with Dixie? I mean Loretta?" Under the stress of this call, I couldn't keep all her names straight.

With a deep breath, Barbara paused and responded, "Mrs. Martinez, we had to contact you now. Ms. Wade isn't expected to make it through the night. Given her familial situation and son's young age, our protocol is to contact the person listed as her emergency contact, and that person, evidently, is you."

"Make it through the night?" I repeated to myself. A foreboding weight landed on my shoulders and started to take my breath. My impatience was replaced with a somber panic. "I'm not familiar with Dixie's health situation, but..." Mary interrupted with regret and calmly said, "That's all I can share over the phone."

At that point, I could only sit there silently, trying to process this news. On top of that, I considered what it meant for this woman's son. It wasn't that long ago that I was talking to her at her house. I began to get emotional at the gravity of this situation, which came out of nowhere. I recalled her saying she wasn't feeling well, but she attributed it to everyday stress. Nothing she shared with me alluded to anything so severe or urgent.

"Mrs. Martinez, are you still there?" Mary asked.

I cleared my throat and responded, "I'm sorry, but this is a lot to process all at once."

Mary replied in a reassuring and understanding tone, "I

understand, and I'm sorry. This situation is clearly more complicated than we thought, given that you don't know Mrs. Wade all that well.

I replied, "All that is true, but we don't have time to waste. I'm on my way."

* * *

I COULDN'T REMEMBER the last time I felt like this. I felt like the world was spinning around me, and I was turning in the opposite direction. In minutes, I went from deciding what I'd have for lunch to potentially making decisions about someone's life — someone I'd only ever met and spoken to *once*.

"Now, she's in the hospital, and if I don't get there, Child Services will take her son into the state's custody." My heart went out, and I assumed I could do something to help under the circumstances. I thought, "I'll just pick him up until someone from his family shows up. Surely, someone in their immediate family will be notified and come to his aid."

I glanced down at the time, but all that registered was the importance of making a clearheaded decision. And I couldn't make one of this magnitude without Kinney. "But they're at the airport. Their plane should be in the air by now." I thought. I started the car and spoke my destination into the navigation. "Valley Spring Regional Hospital." While the directions loaded, I texted Kinney a 'mind-blown' emoji. Before I could put the car into drive, his name popped up on the dash touchscreen.

"Hi, Baby! You miss us already?" asked Kinney jokingly. I could hear airport terminal sounds faintly in the background, so they hadn't yet boarded the plane. I was relieved.

"You are not going to believe this mess," I said. The tone in his deep voice turned concerned but more curious than panicked. "O.K... Well, what's going on?" he asked.

"I don't have much time, but I received a call from the Valley

Spring Hospital asking me if I knew a woman named Loretta Wade. I didn't know anyone by the name, but then they told me that Loretta Wade is Dixie."

Kinney didn't seem to grasp the revelation. I clarified, "... who we know as Luke's mom." Kinney tried to remember, "Luke? Hmm, which kid is that?"

Nick and Noel overheard their father mention Luke's name. Both raised their heads from their devices and looked at one another, catching Kinney's watchful eye. Nick looked at Kinney with an expression that could only be read as 'uh-oh,' which immediately jogged Kinney's memory. "Oh yeah, right... Luke. One of Nick's little homies - the one who comes to trampoline without a shirt." Noel giggled while Nick responded with a frown at the description. I also chuckled a bit and confirmed he had the right kid. "Yes, that one - with the black hair and dark eyes! Chunky, but cute..."

I could hear the smirk on Kinney's face as he replied. "Yeah, the one Nick said he was 'babysitting' when we didn't know where the hell he was that day. So, what about him – is he OK? Did he get into some trouble or something?"

"I'll get to that in a second, but first, let me tell you about Dixie," I said. Kinney exclaimed, "Oh wait! I remember. You went over there and talked to her a couple of weeks back after that babysitting incident."

"That's not what I went over there for, but close enough." I could tell this was one of those 'see, I was listening...' moments that he (and all good husbands) loved to relish. I continued, "She told me she wasn't feeling well but said it was stress... The hospital just told me that Dixie isn't expected to make it through the night."

Kinney paused and lowered his voice to respond, "Oh no, Naomi. That's awful. But... why... how did the hospital call you?!" he asked quizzically.

"That's what I'm saying. She put me down as her emergency

contact, but that's not all." I went on to give him the full rundown as I drove. From Kinney's voice, I knew the look on his face without seeing it. He scowled in a low whisper, "What in the world!? She's got some life-threatening illness, and they are calling you? Where are her next of kin? Luke's dad? Why aren't they telling you more?"

I replied, "Great questions, but that's all I know, and that's exactly what I'm trying to figure out. I'm headed to Valley Spring now."

"Ugh, Valley Spring!? You've got to be kidding me." Kinney's visceral reaction was a response to Valley Spring's legacy as a sundown town back in the day. Times had changed since then, and the hospital was the area's premier research and teaching hospital. But, for non-white families that have grown up in the Middleton metro area, Valley Spring was a small town to be avoided.

"Kinney, Child Services is on the way there right now to get Luke." Kinney knew precisely what that could mean for kids. "I told the social worker I was coming to the hospital to straighten this out." My voice started to break, and I felt the emotions swelling inside. "We have to get him. You know that boy is terrified, and if he comes home with me, he can stay overnight until I figure something out." I continued, "She must have family members. I saw pictures of them at her house that day. They probably don't know what's going on with her yet. I just..."

My voice trailed off, and Kinney gently finished my sentence. "You just want to do the right thing." Knowing we were aligned gave me a moment of relief. I nodded and said, "Okay, we're on the same page. I'll bring him home so that he isn't placed in the system before someone in the family can get him."

"Yep, that's a good idea," Kinney said. "And we'll be home when you get there."

"Wait! What? Oh no, you all board that plane and get out of

here. Your flight should have been in the air by now anyway!" I reassured Kinney that this would all be sorted out by the end of the week and that I would see them at his father's villa next week as planned. Before I ended the call, Kinney called the boys to the row of seats he and Kinsey were camped at within the terminal.

"Okay, everyone," he whispered, "tell Mom she's the greatest and how much we love her. One. Two..." On three, a chorus of noisy, little voices (and Kinney's slight laughter) filled the cabin of my car and my heart, too. It certainly helped break the monotony of my drive, but all too soon, my mind returned to the reasons I was making this drive in the first place—Dixie and Luke.

CHAPTER 5

I was quite familiar with the body's physical reactions to stress. Adrenaline kicks in, and once that happens, breathing becomes shallow, heart rate increases, muscle groups tighten with tension, and so on. My research identified that some people, like career military, first responders, action sports athletes, and doctors, found comfort in highly stressful situations.

As a psychiatrist, driving to the hospital felt like going to work in the early days of my career, and it was calming to a certain degree. Valley Spring Regional Hospital is a famously large research and teaching complex. Seeing the dozens of hospital buildings from the highway, the emergency vehicles, and the crosswalks filled with medical professionals and patients coming and going helped me center despite being in one of the most historically racist places in our state.

Middleton was a sprawling network of communities and municipalities. We lived in Wallace, a well-known and relatively cosmopolitan part of the Middleton metroplex. Valley Spring is also part of the Middleton metroplex, but it's very different from our part of town.

Once upon a time, Valley Spring was the home of a major steel plant that employed most of the community's residents. When steel production increasingly moved offshore, the community suffered. Rather than blaming that on big business and changes in the global economy, Valley Springers blamed their troubles on liberals, foreigners, affirmative action, and the wealthy. I pretty much checked all of those boxes. And if that weren't enough, for the better part of the last 200 years, being here while Black, Brown, or otherwise in Valley Spring was literally a crime. If you grew up in Middleton during the Jim Crow era, you knew better than to be there after sundown, and you probably told your children horror stories about 'The Valley' and 'Valley Springers' to keep them away from that area and ultimately safe. So, while times have changed a bit, the ghosts of this town's racist legacy live on. You can feel it when you drive past the rundown homes, blighted storefronts, and poorly maintained boulevards. Again, it was a far cry from the admittedly elite and pristine suburb where we reside (despite being a short, thirty-minute drive down the highway).

I parked the car and exited the multilevel structure to the bustle of Middleton's largest medical complex. It snapped me back into business mode as I neared the hospital entrance. While I wasn't sure what to expect once I arrived, I felt more prepared to address this situation head-on because hospital settings used to be my everyday life.

I felt the need to move fast, given that the social worker had already called Child Services. "If I'm going to help this kid, I better hustle." Once in the hospital lobby, I realized I didn't know where to go. "I believe she mentioned the fourth floor," I thought out loud. There was a directory on the wall that I quickly scanned to find the elevators. Looking at the guide, I noticed that the fourth floor housed the medical center's oncology and cancer care services. I entered and pressed the fourth-floor button with a growing dread and uncertainty.

When the elevator doors opened, I entered a large foyer with several modern art pieces between office doors before reaching the receptionist. I looked around to orient myself, but it didn't feel like a hospital anymore. "Maybe I pressed the wrong button," I thought as the elevator door closed. Before taking my first steps toward the nurse's station, a man's voice drawled out from across the foyer, "Can I help you?"

Considering this was Valley Spring, an innocent question like, 'Can I help you?' might actually mean, "Explain what you are doing here." I didn't assume the worst and kept an open mind, but I was certainly prepared (just like the nineteen-year-old version of myself).

I turned around to find a plainly dressed man, who I guessed to be in his late fifties or early sixties by the wrinkles in his forehead and his nondescript New Balance shoes. His Southern drawl couldn't mask his kind eyes and friendly smile. "I had the same reaction as you the first time I came to this floor a few months back. Nobody wants to be here, but at least they try to make it comfortable." He must have noticed how confused and out of sorts I seemed when I exited the elevator, and his words confirmed that I was indeed in the right place.

I replied, "Yes, it's quite a space...maybe you can help me. I'm looking for Mary Litzen's office?"

"Oh sure," he said. "Her office is on the right—third door just there." As he pointed me in the right direction, I thanked him and walked toward the door. I didn't fully process the expression on his face, but it was as if he knew something heavy was going on.

As I approached the third door on the right, I could hear Mary talking to someone on speaker phone, and pretty clearly as well. The office wasn't small, but the acoustics made it easy for sounds to travel. I tapped on the door before opening it and sticking my head in to ensure the coast was clear. Mary signaled me with her hand, indicating she needed a moment to finish her call. I gave her a nod of understanding and pulled her door closed. I took a seat, but I could hear everything outside the door.

"Yes, I think Mrs. Martinez is here now, and we'll get her paperwork started..." The conversation went quiet for a few moments. Mary must have taken the phone off speaker mode after I ducked my head in. I then heard her reply," Well, she's only had a few minutes to consider this, and now that she's here, I understand why she was confused about the whole contact thing."

Initially, I thought, "Exactly, thank you for spending a moment in my shoes." Seconds later, I replayed the '...now that she's here, I understand...' part and something on my radar started to blip.

I was only outside Mary's office for a few minutes before she opened the door to signal me in. She knew who I was and extended her hand warmly.

"Hi, Mary. I am Dr. Naomi Martinez. We spoke on the phone regarding Loretta Wade and her son." Her face announced a combination of relief and hurry as she perked up, and her voice hit a higher pitch.

"Yes, yes! Let me take you to her room. Barbara will meet us there as well."

"Okay, no problem," I said. I hadn't planned what to say or do when I saw her. I just felt like I would observe the situation first and then ask questions later if there was time. As we walked to Loretta's room, Mary asked a few questions. "So, you mentioned on the phone that you did not know Loretta?" she clarified with a concerned tone and look.

"Yes, that is correct. I only met her once a few days back. Several kids in the neighborhood come over and play or swim in our backyard, especially when school's out, but we don't know all of them by name." Mary understood and was even more puzzled as we neared a hospital room with the door cracked open. We walked into Loretta's room. A woman in a floral dress sat beside Dixie's bed, texting on her phone.

She didn't look up from her phone as we stepped in.

Looking to the left, I saw Dixie, aka Loretta, lying in bed, appearing fragile and exhausted. "Yes, that's Dixie, alright," I thought. A mix of emotions overcame me: sadness and compassion, but an investigative curiosity took me. Things in this room weren't adding up for some reason. The woman in the dress finally looked up from her phone to see Mary and I standing there. Her reaction seemed startled and defensive as she rose from her chair.

"Charlotte, please, no need to be alarmed," Mary said. "This is Dr. Naomi Martinez."

Charlotte's expression was blank. After an awkward pause, Mary continued, "Dr. Martinez is the woman your sister listed as her emergency contact. "Dr. Martinez, this is Charlotte, Loretta's sister."

I immediately started thinking about what Dixie told me about her family, the only time we talked. Charlotte had a bizarre look on her face. It was as if she were searching for an answer to a question she couldn't quite phrase.

"So, Dixie put you down as her emergency contact?" she said with a doubtful, disapproving tone. By the way she kept looking at me, I could tell she was expecting anyone else but me — perhaps a white Naomi. But a well-dressed, Black woman introduced as a doctor?! It must have been overwhelming for this Charlotte, who I assumed to be a true Valley Springer at heart.

"Apparently, she did," I responded firmly as I looked into her eyes with zero intimidation. "Trust me, Charlotte, I'm just as surprised as you are."

We all stood there for a few awkward moments, looking at each other. I decided that I was done talking with her for the time being. Under the circumstances, I wasn't fond of the negative energy I felt from Charlotte. Here I am, rushing to the hospital for a stranger essentially, and she's sitting here nonchalant and unappreciative. It rubbed me the wrong way and reminded me of things Dixie mentioned during our conversation a couple of weeks ago.

I turned toward the bed where Dixie was lying. She looked so helpless. The tubes and bags of fluid, the monitors beeping, and the pile of blankets covering her from toe to chin to keep her warm. Her face was pale and skeleton-like. I was shocked by how much weight she'd lost since the last time I saw her. I turned to Mary and said, "I had no idea…"

Mary replied, "Yes, the care team has been giving her morphine to keep her comfortable." Charlotte stood with her arms folded, watching my every move, but said nothing. Just then, I remembered I was there to pick up Luke. "This is just awful. Luke must be having a difficult time with all of this. Where is he?" I asked.

Mary looked at Charlotte, and Charlotte looked at Mary. "Wait, why are you all looking at each other? Did Child Services already pick him up?!? I got here as soon as I could."

"No, they haven't, but I'm not sure where he is," Mary said.

"What do you mean? I'm confused. You said you called Child Services to pick him up."

"Luke is not here," Mary said. "It is standard procedure to call them when someone has no spouse, and the next of kin is underaged. When we contacted you initially, you said you did not know who she was. We had to call Child Services because no one else would take him."

"Charlotte is here. I'm sure she is willing to take her nephew. Right, Charlotte?" I asked.

Mary looked embarrassed and said, "Naomi, *Charlotte* was the one who told me to call Child Services. We had to notify *you* first because *you* were listed as her emergency contact."

Charlotte was standing there and hadn't uttered a word. She was staring at us like we weren't talking about her nephew. I'm not sure whether they noticed, but from the air rushing into my mouth and the saliva about to fall from it, my jaw had clearly hit the floor.

I turned to Charlotte and sternly asked her, "Where is Luke?"

She stood there, looked away from me, and shrugged her shoulders with total ambivalence.

"Do you mean to tell me you have no idea where your nephew is?! Where did you guys expect Child Services to pick him up from?" I asked with horror in my voice.

I glared at Mary and Charlotte. At least Mary seemed to grasp how bad this situation was and how much worse this gaffe made things look."I...I...did not know," Mary said. She turned to Charlotte.

"I assumed he was with you. Where exactly is the child?" Again, Charlotte shrugged her shoulders and looked down at her phone as if she had more important things to tend to. Dixie's cousin-sister—or whatever the relation—acted like an emotionless robot.

This whole fiasco had gotten on my last nerve and begun to piss me off. "This mess is going nowhere, and now a child is missing. If the shoe were on the other foot, and I was Charlotte, the hospital would have called Child Services *on me*," I thought.

I paused to gather myself and refocus on the situation. "Let's try a different line of questioning. How long has Dixie been here in the hospital?"

"About a week or so," Mary said.

"Has anyone else been here?"

"No, not to my knowledge," Mary replied.

"How did you know she was here, Charlotte?" I asked, bringing her back into the conversation.

"Cause I'm the one who brought her here," Charlotte replied snarkily.

"Okay, *now* the robot has words," I thought.

29

"Well, did you see Luke when you picked her up from the house?

Charlotte responded, "Yeah, he was outside playing in the front yard or whatever. I told him we'd be back, and he kept on playing. Trust me, that boy has been taking care of himself for years—he's fine."

"So, Luke has no idea that his mom is here, and you left him alone, unattended, for days?!?" I asked. Clearly, my question did not compute as Charlotte stuttered, "I'm-I'm...not sure."

Mary interjected with total shock, "Wait! When you brought Dixie here, Luke wasn't with you?"

I looked at both of them with a disapproving scowl as Charlotte replied, "No..."

Again, awkward silence filled the room. I wondered if Dixie could hear this and how furious I'd be if I were her. But how 'out of it' was she when Charlotte took her to the hospital to not bring Luke?

I stared at Mary and Charlotte for a minute, then broke the silence by asking, "Have you been back to Dixie's since you...?" Before I finished asking, she was nodding her head no, possibly realizing for the first time how bad this made her look.

Mary, with an expression that looked as if she'd sucked a lemon, erupted, "Charlotte, the last time you saw Luke was five days ago..."

I interjected, "...and he has no idea what is happening with his mother?!?" I tried to take the judgmental tone out of my voice to coax a few more answers from Charlotte, the child-neglecting robot. I asked Charlotte if she had notified any other family members, and she said she hadn't. Charlotte's expression returned to the same robotic stoicism she had when we came into the room minutes ago.

The thought of this young kid being home alone for an entire week stunned and terrified me. "It's been a week, and this woman might not make it through the night. Her sister hasn't told any of their other family members what is happening. And someone (apparently me) desperately needs to find Luke and ensure he's alright," I imagined.

I turned to a teary-eyed Mary standing in the corner, documenting the details of this exchange on her clipboard. I told her I would go by Dixie's house to see if Luke was home. Her embarrassment was evident as she nodded. Apologetically, she told me to contact her anytime if I needed anything while checking on Luke. I thanked her and rushed out of the room.

On my way out, I caught a glimpse of the older gentleman who greeted me. He put his hand over his heart and pointed in my direction. I gave him an appreciative nod as I hurried to the elevator and back to my car.

CHAPTER 6

I recall thinking it was good to get out of dodge and head back towards my part of Middleton. It was full of attractive neighborhoods and beautiful green spaces for relaxation and recreation. We lived in Wallace, an economically well-off suburb in Middleton that bordered a massive outdoor park bearing the same name.

Wallace Park, roughly the same size as New York's Central Park, separated Wallace from two neighboring communities—Randall Heights and Oakmont, which were more densely populated and socioeconomically diverse. On any given day, you'd find people old and young doing their things, making our part of Middleton feel more alive and welcoming. In that way, Wallace Park was like an oasis in an otherwise homogenous, midwestern desert.

Our subdivision was impressive, even by Wallace's economically exclusive standards. It wasn't uncommon for people to drive past our homes to gawk. Properties were costly, but for the money, we had every amenity we wanted. Seeing the fruits of our labor when we pulled up was rewarding. The one hundred or so families that call this place home pride themselves on being a close-knit community. I'll admit that some of them are too curious, self-assured, and gossipy for my taste, but I will say they take their neighborhood, investments, and wine very seriously.

Our sons were adventurous, but we were cautious about how far they could venture into the park without one of us and certainly how late they could play outdoors. The park's southern end was nearest to us, hosting several playing fields and courts. Many of the surrounding area's kids gathered here, especially when school was out. When the kids were not at the park, you'd likely find them at each other's houses. This was especially true for us because we had a large backyard with a play area for Kinsey, a trampoline for the boys, and a heated pool for Kinney and me.

I suppose that's where this tale begins. Less than two weeks ago...

* * *

LIKE ANY ATTENTIVE PARENT, I watched my and any kids visiting our house. I paid attention to them close enough to recognize the regulars. I could remember appearances without fail, but I didn't even attempt to keep their names straight.

This summer, I noticed one kid who seemed to be here more regularly than the other children. I wasn't sure if he lived in Wallace, but by the looks of him, I had severe doubts. He had thick, coal-black hair past his shoulders and looked slightly younger than the twins, so I'd have put him at seven or eight years old. I'd rarely seen him with a shirt on, but Middleton's heat probably feels as close to hell as you can get during summer. I could see the dried-up streaks of dirt across his forehead and down the sides of his face from our dining room patio.

"Hi, are Nick and Noel home?" the shirtless little boy asked.

He reminded me of the cartoon Tarzan, shirtless with all that hair scattered over his head.

"They went to the store with their dad for me, but they should be back any minute now."

"Can I play on the trampoline until they come home?" he asked. I nodded that he could.

"Cool! Can I have some water?"

It would have seemed like an odd question, but I usually give out bottles of water, and sometimes popsicles, to the kids who come over to play in our backyard. I try to help the kids stay hydrated, and it keeps them from knocking on my door every few minutes.

"Sure, hold on." I returned with ice-cold water and a popsicle, too. He looked at me with a big smile and nodded in contentment.

"Hey, you're a good, nice mom," he said, all bright-eyed.

"Why, thank you."

He took a sip of water and said, "I think my mom is sick." I figured I did not hear him correctly because he was smiling when he said it.

"I'm sorry, what did you say?" I asked.

He repeated, "I dunno. My mom is sick, but I guess she'll be okay. I dunno." He shrugged his shoulders and skipped toward the trampoline.

I wasn't going to interrogate this little boy, but who the hell says that and then skips off to play? I've never met him or his parents, and by the looks of it, he probably lives on the far side of the park. "Probably lives in Oakmont, but that's a fairly long way from home for a kid this young," I thought as I watched him jump and bounce. All I could tell you is that he was a familiar face. Nick and Noel would host at least six or seven other regulars in our backyard, just like this little guy. Two things stood out—it was the first time that this young, Tarzan look-alike ever said anything close to a 'thank you,' and none of their other friends have dared to come over without the boys, much less come into the backyard on their own.

I thought it was weird for him to randomly blurt out his mom's condition—no provocation, context, or detail. More interesting was that he was so nonchalant about it - he was smiling, which may have been the reaction to quenching his thirst, the popsicle, or that I allowed him to play on the trampoline. Regardless, it didn't sync up in my mind. I said a quick prayer that whatever was going on in this kid's life would have God's hands on it and continued to watch him for a few more minutes before the boys arrived with their Dad.

Several hours had passed, and it was just about nightfall. I was sure the kids had come in from playing, and I was in our conservatory. It's one of my favorite rooms for reading, reflecting, or working when the home office won't do. It's full of greenery, has a pleasant view of the front yard, and looks into the nearby park.

I was reading and sipping a glass of Laphroaig when I heard someone honking their horn outside. It was odd to hear a car horn this close to the house at that hour. I didn't think much of it until the honking continued. "That's not a coincidence," I thought, and I went to my front door to see who was out there making all this noise. I looked out and saw an older, blue pickup truck near the entrance of our driveway. When I opened the front door, the alarm sensor beeped, getting everyone's attention. Kinney stood at the top of the foyer with an annoyed Kinsey. "What's going on out there, Mom? It's too late for more friends!" she said.

I couldn't argue with that. I popped my head out the front door to get a better look. I squinted to make out the person inside this noisy vehicle. The passenger side window lowered, and I saw a hand waving at me, then what appeared to be a woman smiling. I turned to the family and said, "Looks like someone's mom. I've got it."

Kinney grabbed Kinsey's hand and headed toward her room. I assumed the boys were too busy with their regularly scheduled programming (e.g., video gaming) to come and see what was going on. I stepped onto our porch and motioned the visitor to enter the driveway. I cautiously approached the vehicle but noticed Kinney and Kinsey watching guard from her bedroom window, which looked down onto the driveway.

"Hi, is Luke here?" the woman asked.

Still annoyed by the honking, I replied, "Oh, I'm sorry, I think you might have the wrong house. There are no children here but mine. A few were here playing earlier, but I'm afraid they all left before dark."

The woman explained, "Luke's friends with your son Nick, and they hang out and play. I thought he might be over here. I'm his mom, of course, not just some random woman looking for kids," she laughed awkwardly trying to hide her worry and embarrassment. I played along by smiling, but my inner voices had other, less savory things to say.

"No, of course. You're just trying to find him. Like I said, some kids were here earlier, but they all left some time ago. Sorry, I wish I could be of more help."

She smiled politely. "Okay, I'm sorry for bothering you. It's not the first time I've had to find him this close to dark. I'm sure he's fine. He's probably home now, I'll bet! Thanks again."

I gestured goodbye as the woman backed down the driveway, and I headed back into the house. I had no idea which little boy she was talking about, but I was confident they had all left. With my zen vibe disrupted, I finished my scotch in a swallow and took my glass to the kitchen. I looked out the kitchen window into the backyard and saw a pair of figures near the trampoline. I opened the patio door and went toward them.

"Hey, what are you guys doing back here? I asked. "I thought you were inside playing Madden."

Nick replied, "Noel is. It's just me and Luke talking."

36

I huffed, "It's getting dark and late, and Nick, you know better!" I looked at the other little boy. Of course, it's the kid from earlier—Tarzan Jr. "Oh, so you're Luke. Well, your mom was just here looking for you. Didn't you guys hear someone out front honking?" They looked at each other, but neither seemed to hear anything. "Okay, well, time's up, guys. Time to go home," I said.

Nick asked, "Mom, can we give Luke a ride?" Before I could reply, Luke said, "Nope, I'm okay. I can get home faster through the park. I do it all the time. Bye, Nick. Bye, Nick's mom."

And just like that, he was on his way.

That exchange gave me pause, especially after his mother said that looking for him after dark was common.

I just shook my head and escorted Nick toward the patio by his shoulder. "You little… I didn't even know you were out here playing in the dark! I should ground you. You're lucky to be leaving in a week, or I would…" I motioned as if I were going to get him.

He took off running and laughing and ran into the house a few steps ahead of me. Before he ran up the stairs, I said, "Nicky, do you have Luke's phone number? You call him and make sure he got home safely."

"Okay, Mom," he replied. I made my way to the bedroom and called it a night.

CHAPTER 7

y alarm went off the next morning, and I felt slightly hungover. A well-aged, single malt can do that, though. I went to sleep replaying the strange exchange I had with Luke yesterday afternoon when he told me about his mom. Then, I tried to piece together what he said to the woman in our driveway looking for him. It bothered me all that morning. So, after finishing my usual morning news routine, reading emails, and reviewing my calendar, I detoured into the conservatory to focus and pray.

When something weighs heavy on my spirit, a good, spiritual dialogue with the maker helps me feel better. Sure, there are cliches like, "...Every challenge is an opportunity, and God doesn't give us anything we can't handle." And "...It's not a matter of winning or losing; only a matter of living and learning." But, I toss in parts of the serenity prayer plus my humble requests for guidance, patience, protection, and resilience. My prayers are for me sometimes, but usually for Kinney and the kids. No matter what I ask or confess, those moments of focused connection generally do the trick. But this time was a bit different. I didn't receive the peace of mind I hoped for, but I did receive clarity.

"I have to go to Luke's house and talk to his mom about our conversation." Only then would I be able to rest the nagging suspicion weighing on me. I made a small pot of Esmeralda, Panama's finest blend, in my opinion, to help me wrestle with the idea of going over to this woman's house. My inner voices had varying views on the subject.

"What are you thinking, Naomi? You don't know them like that. Go back to bed."

Another said, "Relax. You are blowing this out of proportion. He's just a kid you see in the backyard occasionally."

Another of my inner voices agreed, "She may not even be sick. Kids do say the darnedest things, right?"

I consciously wondered if he and Nick had talked about his mom. "I should probably ask Nick, but I don't want him concerned if they haven't."

Then my bougie voice chimed in with her opinion. "Did she *honk* in front of my house?!? We knock on doors if we come to someone's home. And never unannounced! Shameful."

This jury of inner voices seemed unanimous, but I overruled them - my right as chief justice in the court of Naomi. "Trust your instincts and go on over there. Nick can tell you where Luke lives, and you can go over there whenever your heart says so." With that, I was decided. I went upstairs and started getting myself together. Kinney looked at me from the bed as I finished getting dressed.

"You up already, baby? It's Saturday."

"Just have something to do quickly, but it shouldn't take long. You keep resting." I kissed him and headed to the boys' room. I could tell they were still sleeping.

"Nicky?" I whispered. "I need to go over to Luke's house. Can you tell me where he lives?"

The boys explored the entire park with their scout troop and learned impressive navigational skills. Nick gave me great detail without fully opening his eyes to engage me.

"So, let me run it back. Head through the park, towards the courts, and cross the street. Go down three blocks to a cul-de-sac on the Oakmont side. The gray house just past the school, but if I get to the large fountain, I've gone too far, correct?"

"Mm-hmm," Nick groaned as he turned over. I kissed him on his forehead. Then, I left on foot through the park to Luke's house.

* * *

WALLACE PARK IS HUGE, but the paths are wide and well-traveled. If I had considered it too dangerous, I wouldn't have let Luke go alone last night after dusk. People were already out walking their dogs and going for morning jogs. I was busy enough with the kids every morning that I felt well-exercised by the time I got them out the door! Still, I had a tiny sense of excitement and accomplishment from being in the morning air, 'getting my steps.'

As the celebration of my walk was replaced with mouth breathing and muscle aches, I tried to rationalize what I was doing. I couldn't pinpoint the exact reason I needed to make this trek. I suppose I was answering some motherly call of duty that couldn't be ignored, right? Maybe I was being nosy, like the neighbors I so often criticize. I knew one thing: I should have driven!

Being the trooper I am, I returned to thinking about what I would say when I showed up at their door unannounced. "At least I wouldn't be out front honking..." I thought jokingly.

Based on Nick's directions, I knew I was getting close. Good thing, because I was really 'feeling the burn' as they say. As I entered the cul-de-sac, I could see the same blue truck that visited my house last night. As I got closer, I was even more sure

I was in the right place. A gray, two-story home with black shutters on the windows. These homes weren't nearly as palatial or stately as the ones on our side of the park, but they were nicer than my inner voices thought they'd be.

As I walked up their modest driveway, I started to feel like I should turn around. "I have no idea what to say. What if this little boy is exaggerating his mother's situation? She could have the flu or something. Kids have wild imaginations." It sounded like my coffee conversation all over again, but I followed my heart and started up their porch.

The last steps were the hardest. The sun was already out and blazing, and I'd just walked what seemed like miles, but my palms were the only thing sweating. "My palms never sweat. This is a nervous reaction. You're anxious, and that's normal under the circumstances," I counseled myself.

"You're not the type of person to just show up on a stranger's doorstep (unless it's for a kid's fundraiser or trick-or-treating), but this was WAY different," quipped one of my voices.

"Well, I'm here, and there is no turning back now," I said to my jury of inner voices. I spent too much time pondering the what-ifs and not enough time thinking about what I would say.

"Screw it, here goes nothing." I knocked on the door.

I stood there. I waited. The seconds felt like minutes. There was no answer. I leaned my ear closer to the door to check for sounds of movement on the other side.

Nothing.

"Told you! You did it. Get out of here before someone calls the cops on you or something."

"Shush," I thought. Against my inner voice's recommendation, I knocked again, this time a bit longer, and waited a few more seconds.

Still no answer.

"Maybe she is a late sleeper or in the shower, and she can't hear me knocking," I told myself. My dedication to this was waning anyway. All I needed was an excuse.

I let the screen door go and turned to leave. Before relief could set in, I heard the door open behind me.

It was as if the chorus of doubt in my mind started booing.

"No!"

"We were so close!"

"Aww, hell naw."

Then, I heard her voice. I took a deep breath, fixed my expression, and turned around. "Hey, lady!" the middle-aged woman said with a big smile. "You're Nick's mom! Please, come on in!"

CHAPTER 8

*H*ave you ever met someone whose smile made you smile instantly? Luke's mom had that exact thing — warm, inviting, and sweet. I smiled from ear to ear, not knowing what to say or do next. Yes, I talked to people for a living, so one would appropriately conclude that I'd be more prepared, or minimally, in my comfort zone in situations like this one. But, keep in mind, my patients come with a file containing background information, making initial meet and greets a cinch. But for this one, I had to be more investigative and wing it. I told myself, "The agenda is to have no agenda. Stick to the small talk and let the conversation go where it will."

"Hi, my name is Naomi Martinez. I believe you came to my house the other day looking for your son?"

"Yes!" she responded with excitement in her voice. As she invited me into her spacious home, for reasons I couldn't explain, it felt cold and temporary. "I never have company over," she said. "Can I offer you a drink of water?"

"That would be great," I said, even though I was not thirsty. Her stepping away would give me a few extra moments to prepare my thoughts. I didn't want to seem more intrusive than

I already felt, but I still wasn't sure if this kid was exaggerating, and I had to suss out the truth as best I could.

As she went for water, I looked around a bit. The walls had wood paneling, and the floor was tile. "Awful in the winter," I thought. On top of that, the furniture was very dated, like someone considerably older might have been living there with her (or her and Luke with them). I knew one thing — I hadn't seen a sofa and loveseat with checkered, wool upholstery like that since childhood and maybe at my grandparent's house. Mid-century modern? Maybe, but there wasn't much of a theme beyond those pieces.

It was neither here nor there, but I couldn't help noticing their living space as I tried to piece things together. The walls only hosted a few pictures - one with her and Luke when he was a baby, another with an elderly lady I'd guessed was probably her mother, and a framed portrait of Jesus (the European one, not the biblical description one). Aside from that, the house was neat but could have used a dusting, according to my discerning eye. I concluded that Luke and his mom probably faced some economic challenges, but otherwise, things seemed okay.

She returned from the kitchen with two glasses of water. We sat down, and she put my drink on the table before me. She asked kindly, "What brings you over this beautiful morning?" So much for small talk...

"Well, the other day, Luke was at my house playing in my backyard with the other children, and I overheard him mention to the other kids that his mother was sick." I know that's not the way it went exactly, but that's how I was comfortable explaining it to her.

"I wanted to check on you and see if you needed anything. I'm actually a psychiatrist, and I thought I would extend my services to you if you ever needed to talk. The first visit would be free of charge." I hoped that particular tidbit of information would establish trust between her and me. "If she wanted me to know any more details about her health, she ought to be more comfortable disclosing them," I mused.

She took a drink of water and smiled politely before responding. "Well, thank you for coming all this way and checking on me. That was very thoughtful of you." I noticed her smile diminish a bit. "He's right. I am not feeling well these days. But it's just stress. Trying to get things on the right track, I just started a new job at the school..."

I nodded gently, but I didn't press her on anything. I just let her talk a bit longer about her job. She elaborated on a few other things but nothing about being ill. After several minutes of oratory, she paused. She looked at me and said, "Now, I see where your sons get their kindness from."

"Oh, well, thank you," I said with a bit of surprise. "So, you've spent time with my boys?" I asked.

She smiled. "Well, no, but I know they are good kids." Her response didn't answer my question. I wouldn't have guessed that she knew the twins well enough to speak so highly of their character. They're just ten-year-olds, after all.

"You seem *really* familiar... How do you know them so well?" I asked casually, but my interest in her answer was quite serious. She picked up on my signal and replied, "They have been a blessing for me and Luke since I started that new job."

Now, she had my undivided attention. I leaned forward and took a sip of the water she'd brought. I was careful, ensuring my skin didn't contact this sofa, as I was sure the stiff wool fabric would scratch my arm and cause me to break out.

"What do you mean *blessing*?" I asked.

"Luke is always talking about how nice your sons are. Nick and Noel, this. Nick and Noel, that. They always pick me for their teams when no one else will," she said, imitating his voice and enthusiasm.

I expressed my relief with a laugh, but I still had an inquisition in my tone. "Oh, okay! That makes a little more sense. I've always taught them to be kind and treat others as they would want to be treated. But, you mentioned your new job as well..." She took the cue to elaborate, as I hoped she would.

"Right! Right. So, I started a new job a few months ago," she said, "and I didn't have anyone to watch Luke after school for an hour or two while I finished work. He claimed he was afraid to stay home by himself, and your son Nick said he would stay here at the house with him or play outside together until I got home."

I sat and calmly listened to her explain, but I was shocked to hear that Nick was doing this. I'd deal with that later, but I took another sip of water before asking, "Where is Luke's father?"

The question struck a nerve because she rolled her eyes in disgust, stood up, and started pacing around the room. There must be quite a story there, and I could tell by her body language and facial expressions that it wasn't a happy one.

I thought her reaction was strange, but it wasn't anything I couldn't handle.

"Ok... come back, come back." I coaxed her back to the loveseat to finish our chat.

"Is there anyone else's house he can go to with or an adult that could come by and watch him while you work? No family nearby or something?" I asked.

While Luke's mother seemed very lovely, being 'nice' didn't have anything to do with the quality of her judgment. I thought, "Hello, my son is ten. Your son is seven or eight at best. I don't leave my children at home unattended like that, so there's no way I'd sign off on either of them 'babysitting.'" She would need to find a permanent solution for her childcare problem because Nick and Noel wouldn't be watching any kids besides their sister on my watch.

"I don't have any family," she said softly. "It's just me and Luke." Judging by her tone, I knew she meant something else. I just looked at her, and after a few seconds, she elaborated. "I

46

have a couple of siblings I haven't seen for a while because my relationship with the family isn't good. The last time I saw them, not only did my cousin slap me in the face, but they took a vote to sell the house we were living in with my aunt; God rest her soul."

"Jeez, this woman has been through a lot," I thought. She continued, "My mom died when I was very young. My brother, and I went to live with her sister. My aunt had a daughter and a son who were a few years older than me — Kyle and Charlotte," she growled, signaling her disdain for the pair.

"Although they're my cousins, we were raised like siblings," she said. "My aunt became ill, and I was the one that took care of her - without any support from my cousins. A few days after she passed, Kyle and Charlotte arrived at the house with a freakin' realtor," she said in frustration. "I had no idea they were selling the house. Especially so soon after her death. I mean, WTF, we hadn't even had her funeral yet!?!"

She was still mourning, obviously, but the house situation added insult to injury.

"My god, that must have been hard for you. That's just terrible. I'm very sorry for your loss." I knew it wasn't much comfort coming from a stranger, but she graciously received my sentiment all the same.

"Thank you," she said, with a warm smile as she continued her story.

"I was told the house was being sold and that Luke and I needed to find another place to live. I pleaded with them to let us stay another month because we had nowhere to go on such short notice. I had no job then because I was caring for my aunt, but she was THEIR mom! They never even helped me with her," she said sadly.

"They told me that wasn't their problem, and I just needed to move out or else. Charlotte said they took a vote and unanimously agreed to sell the house, pay the back taxes, and split whatever was left. My aunt didn't have much, but it was wrong for them to do her like that. They just came and grabbed her things from the home like it was nothing. Like she was nothing..."

Her voice shook with frustration as she tried to hold back her tears. "That's when I told them to get out of the house. Jennifer, Charlotte's brute of a daughter, told me it was not my house. We went back and forth, got in each other's faces, and she slapped me!"

Nothing about my walk prepared me for the soap opera drama she narrated from that terrible, plaid chair. But it was gripping! All I could think was how truly dysfunctional this family must have been. I couldn't imagine a niece or nephew of mine raising their hand and slapping one of their elders. But I also couldn't imagine a family having a secret vote to sell a house off from under their kin, especially when they have a small child in tow. "Sometimes truth is stranger than fiction," I said to myself.

As captivating as her story was, it was cringingly messy. I couldn't help but feel sorry for her because she seemed lovely — pretty face, friendly smile, and petite stature. As far as I could tell, she seemed to have a decent sense of humor. She struck me as sweet and non-confrontational but showed some impulsivity in the few minutes we'd shared. To have her family treat her and her son like crap and still manage to grin suggested that she had resilience. But, I sensed a lot of damage behind her warm facade. I needed to put one more point of investigation to bed, though: Was this woman really sick or just stressed out? There were signs of psychological and emotional PTSD, but I couldn't discern any physical ailments. Still, it was better to ask than assume.

"So, back to what I overheard your son say yesterday. You are O.K.?" I asked.

She paused and looked at me. A grin slowly emerged on her

face, and she started laughing hard, leaning back on the loveseat with her hands on her legs. She sat up, looked at me, and said, "I'm a mess — I never told you my name, did I?"

Come to think of it, she hadn't. I smiled and said, "No, you didn't, but it's alright. I figured you'd get around to it when you were ready. Maybe sooner than this, but it's fine, right!?"

We both laughed. Given how dire and dark her story had been up to that point, it was refreshing to have a moment of levity.

She extended her hand and announced, "Hello, I'm Dixie."

I stood up, shook her hand firmly, and said, "I'm Naomi." We continued laughing as we exaggerated our handshake. I told her it was a pleasure to meet her, but I needed to start my return trek home. I approached the door and asked, "So, where is Luke this morning? Still in bed?"

"Nope," she said, "He's somewhere running around. He comes and goes as he pleases. I try to parent him, Naomi. I do. I give him structure and everything, but he won't listen to anything I say." She shook her head and confessed, "The other day when I came to your house looking for him... he never came home until around 10 p.m."

"Really?!?" I said with shock. "That is too late for a kid his age to be out and about by himself. He left our house hours before that! I offered to give him a ride, but he insisted on walking home and took off."

"I know, I know. And I'm certain you did," she said. "But sometimes Luke stays outside until midnight playing basketball," she said, pointing to an old basketball hoop in their driveway.

"So much for structure," I said to myself.

Dixie continued, "He's been a handful since he was a baby. When he was a toddler, he would hold his breath when he got upset, and one day, that little monster held it so long that he literally passed out." She told the story with a half-smile, but I could tell she wasn't proud of her parental resume with the boy. I wasn't a specialist in child psychiatry either, but after that anecdote about Luke as a toddler and learning that he regularly ran the streets after dark, my radar was blipping more now than when I came over in the first place.

I felt compelled to ask about his father again as I approached the door. "Dixie, is there any possibility of him spending more time with his dad? Sometimes a male figure can be helpful for young boys with behavior challenges."

"Oh, God, no! Cash is a monster. That fucker... *He's* the one with the behavior challenges." She wasn't smiling or joking this time. Her tone was deadly serious.

"*Cash?*" I asked skeptically. His name was colloquial, to say the least.

"Yep, Luke's sperm donor. He hasn't been a part of Luke's life, and I'll do everything I can to keep it that way... I ran away from him right after Luke came into the world, and I hope he never finds us."

I had heard all I needed to hear, but she continued. "He assaulted me the last time I saw him. This guy has a history of extreme substance abuse and domestic violence charges from abusing all these women, and I was one of them," she said.

My heart went out to her, but the visit started to feel like a mini-series that ran an episode too long. I was standing by the door because I was trying to leave, and she kept talking. I tried to be patient. "Remember, she doesn't get visitors often... Her family is, well, we know all about that now... She needs this outlet. She needs an ear for just a little bit longer." Despite all that, my legs were getting tired from standing, and the walk back would be a little harder now that the temperature had crept up several degrees.

I think she could tell that I was beyond ready to leave. Her tone became apologetic. "I've said too much. I'm sorry. I do that all the time." She dropped her head and mumbled,

"Nobody loves me, Naomi." Her voice was so depleted and sad.

I sighed. Her damage was palpable. I would have preferred having this interaction with some client-patient context as a guardrail — for the patient as much as myself. But again, I wasn't outside my depth.

"I'm sure it might feel that way sometimes, but you know that's not true. You have to love yourself. And then, you must practice that love daily, " I said with a smile.

Dixie nodded and smiled back. "That's the best advice I think I've ever gotten. Are you a therapist or doctor or something? I wouldn't be surprised with that beautiful house of yours."

I assumed she was kidding because I had already told her my occupation, but I smiled. I thought to myself, "Mission accomplished, Naomi. Now, get to steppin'!" On that high note, I intended to make my exit. I turned and took another step through the door towards her front porch, making my departure official.

I got a few more feet towards the yard before she hollered, "You know, you're right! I *won* my battle against breast cancer years ago. What's not to love?!?"

She couldn't see my face, but I grimaced before stopping mid-stride and turning around. Of course, I returned to acknowledge her revelation with the respect it deserved. "Oh, my God, Dixie. You're a cancer survivor, too?" I approached and grabbed her hand. We walked back inside the house and toward that terrible, scratchy couch.

We sat down together. "This couch is the worst, isn't it," she laughed.

"Please, this is mid-century modern, my dear. Very couture." She paused to see if I was being sarcastic, and we both cracked up.

"Dixie.…. Look, you're *here*, and that's what matters," I said.

"It's been hard... life hasn't been kind to me, Naomi. Not by any means," she said.

Holding her hand, I said, "You've come a long way. Remember that. Luke is lucky to have you. Your job is lucky to have you." She looked at me with a faint smile as though she knew I was trying to make her feel better, but her mood was on a downward spiral.

"Dixie," I said in a soft tone. "I'm going to give you the name of a friend of mine. He is a very reputable psychiatrist. I believe he'll be very helpful to you. Do you have a pen and paper? Or, where's your phone?"

"That's probably a great idea. Let me go get it," she said. She stood up and walked into the other room.

I took a deep breath and tried to reset quickly before she returned. I wasn't being disingenuous. I was concerned for her. Dixie was suffering from depression and was either undiagnosed or diagnosed and untreated. I was worried about her being alone in her current state of mind and thought of her little boy's safety as well.

Dixie returned to me with a pen and paper. "Dixie, maybe there is someone we can call to sit with you and Luke? A work friend or significant other, perhaps? As a professional, I'm not sure you should be alone now."

"No, Naomi... I'm fine. It's my normal. There's no one. Nobody loves Dixie. Well, no one but Dixie, I guess." She said it with a smirk on her face. Maybe she was being sarcastic or practicing what I had just preached to her a moment ago. Depression manifests itself that way — the mood swings, the misdirection, and the hurt that sufferers project outward as anger or manipulation. None of what she was doing was unfamiliar. It was textbook, and I was less fearful for her safety after 1) her explanation and 2) her willingness to take my colleague's information.

As I wrote on her paper, I was compelled to express my

empathy for her journey and validate her success in managing through it all. "Anyone would feel overwhelmed, but given what you've survived... You've overcome more than most women face in a lifetime!"

Dixie shrugged her shoulders and began weeping into her hands. I rubbed her shoulder, and the words fell out of my mouth, "Dixie, I love you."

Dixie wiped her tears, looked up at me, and said faintly, "Thank you." Again, I wasn't being disingenuous. I was just being nice. This lady was in a terrible place, and I wanted to lift her spirits.

"Dixie, I'd love to stay, but I must get home. The number I left you... Be sure to give him a call first thing Monday. He is outstanding, and I think you will like him."

She walked me to the door with a smile and promised that she would follow through. After we hugged and parted ways, I walked across the porch and started down the driveway.

"Naomi?"

Dixie called my name as I was walking away.

"Not again, I thought."

"What did you say your last name was?"

"Martinez, I replied loudly." Like most, my last name surprised her, but only for a second. "I'll let Dr. Bernard know that I referred you! Take care, hon!" As I waved goodbye, she stood at her door waving back as I began my journey home.

I remember it all being a lot to take in. The thought of this sad woman and her sad life was all I could think about. "I have to get out of this headspace," I thought as I picked up my pace through the park. Their house had given me an unsettling feeling, one I couldn't quite describe - like there was something unstable and emotionally toxic in the air. Once I left, it was as if I could breathe again.

My mind shifted to the babysitting debacle. Nick certainly wouldn't be 'babysitting' Luke anymore. "C'mon, Nick is a little kid himself," I thought. Plus, I didn't want him exposed to any more of their family dysfunction. "God knows what else was going on with them," I told myself. Sure, everyone has that one unpredictable relative in their family who acts out at reunions, holidays, or BBQs. But, the point is—you know what to expect. More likely than not, you keep them at arm's length because of all the trouble and drama accompanying them.

I couldn't rule out the possibility that *Dixie* was that family member and not the other way around. I sensed three sides to her saga: Dixie's version, her family's version, and somewhere in between, lay the truth of the matter.

I wasn't sure I even wanted the truth. She said she won her fight against breast cancer some years ago, and whatever ailed her now was more psychological and emotional than physical.

"Like I said, mission accomplished." As far as I was concerned, the only thing left to do was nip this babysitting thing in the bud with my little 'St. Nick'.

CHAPTER 9

As I pulled up the driveway to our house, part of my mind was still in disbelief. I suppose I was trying to convince myself that this couldn't be happening. "Charlotte only left this seven-year-old there because someone else—a responsible, caring person—would be there to look after him eventually." I thought, "Surely, this kid hasn't been home alone for a week. No way. No possible, freakin' way."

I couldn't wait to call Kinney and update him on this shit show, but my head was pounding. "Deep breathing won't fix this one. I'm going to need some ibuprofen," I said to myself. I sat my things down in the foyer and headed straight upstairs to the medicine cabinet.

After swallowing a few tablets and changing from my shopping attire, I threw myself on the couch in our family room. I started replaying this situation in my head while the TV played. No matter how many times I replayed the scenario in my mind, I couldn't reconcile it.

I asked myself, "Who lists someone they don't know as an emergency contact, on their deathbed no less, with family in the room!?"

I answered, "Dixie, in this case, but why?"

I replied, "Damn...her support system is so limited that she would prefer a stranger caring for her son? And a Black one at that?!?"

I snapped out of my inner dialogue and concluded that things must have been terrible for her, and they didn't just become that way recently. Things had probably been tough for her and Luke for a long time. Not to mention Charlotte, the robot at the hospital, was no help. I remember Dixie telling me a little about her family that day I went to see her, so I guess I should not be surprised Charlotte was acting the way she did. I'm pretty sure she was expecting someone else. It is comical now that I think back, mainly because I know she is a hot mess.

I resolved to head to Dixie's house, but first, I needed a nap. I was sure that Dixie had made arrangements for Luke to stay with someone before Charlotte took her to the hospital, and I dozed off with that thought in mind.

A couple of hours passed, and I felt much better after having had a chance to rest. I freshened up a bit and drove over to Dixie's house. It was hard to tell whether or not someone was home from the looks of things, so I turned my car off and walked up to the door. I pushed the doorbell but didn't hear anything. Assuming it didn't work, I began knocking. I didn't hear anyone on the other side of the door, but I knocked again anyway—dead silence. I was relieved to think that this seven-year-old wasn't home by himself unattended, but also concerned that I didn't know his whereabouts.

Just as the screen door closed and I turned away, I heard the front door crack open. The relief I briefly felt washed away in an instant. I looked over my shoulder to see a cute little boy wearing a superhero tee shirt and matching underwear. His jet-black hair was scattered over his head while he rubbed his eyes. We stood there for a few seconds, looking at each other. When he recognized me, an innocent smile appeared on his face.

"Hi," he said sleepily. I gathered that I interrupted his nap because I could see red streaks on his face, as though he was lying on something other than a pillow.

I knelt down a bit to make him more comfortable before I spoke. "Hi, Luke. I'm sorry I woke you up. I'm here to check on you and make sure you are doing alright."

"Okay," he said, squinting as he looked at me.

"Do you know who I am?"

"Yes, you're Nick's mom," Luke said.

"That's right! I'm glad you remember. Now, is there someone here in the house with you?" He shook his head from left to right.

"No, it's just me." The words made my stomach turn, and my worst fear for him was confirmed.

"When will someone be home so I can speak with them?" I asked. Luke stood there and shrugged his shoulders, suggesting he didn't know. I was careful with my facial expressions so I wouldn't alarm him, but it was increasingly difficult to hide my feelings.

I asked, "Luke, may I come in, please?" He opened the door wider for me to come inside.

I walked in and looked around. The place looked almost exactly as it did when I visited only a few days back. I asked Luke, "Has anyone been here with you – today or yesterday?"

"My mom was here, but she's gone. I haven't seen her for a long time," he said, walking down a hallway and entering a room. I approached their kitchen, hoping to find any other signs that someone had been there to care for him. I saw cereal and milk on the table, but not much was left. I noticed bread, an empty package of lunch meat, some PB and J on the counter, and a little step stool he must have used to get into the cabinets.

"Luke, when was the last time anyone was here with you?" I said in a louder voice so he could hear me.

"I'm not sure," he said as I heard the toilet flush.

I felt a chill go through my body as it all began to dawn on me. What I feared seemed altogether true. "He has no idea his mom is in the hospital. She's been there for almost an entire week, and he's been fending for himself all that time."

He came into the kitchen where I was standing and approached the table where the cereal and milk were. I asked him, "Luke, when was the last time you saw your mother?"

"A while ago," he said.

"What do you mean?" I asked.

"I don't know, a few days, I guess," he replied.

My heart hit the floor. I wanted to cry and hug this little boy who seemed to be fine on the surface. His hygiene and appearance needed some attention, but for the most part, he seemed okay being home alone. Before I knew it, I said, "Get dressed. You are coming with me." Luke looked surprised but smiled and eagerly ran to his room to put some clothes on.

I smiled at his enthusiasm but felt angry at that moment. I had questions. "Who leaves a little kid home alone for a whole week?! Why wouldn't Charlotte return from the hospital and get him, especially when she knew Dixie would be admitted? How could he have been left here with no one to watch over him? How hadn't anyone living nearby noticed and not called the authorities? I continued imagining how bad this could have wound up when Luke exited his room. He had put on some socks, shoes, and basketball shorts but no shirt. I chuckled but was puzzled that he'd dressed to leave without being fully clothed.

"Where's your shirt?" I asked. He pointed toward the room he had just come out of and started walking toward the kitchen. I went to Luke's room and saw a dresser by the door. In his room was a twin bed with clothes scattered on the floor. There were no decorations, posters, drawings, or anything to indicate that he spends much time here. I was not in the mood to look through his stuff, so I grabbed a relatively clean shirt and headed towards the kitchen. I figured we'd return to get some of his things later, but I wanted out.

When I returned to the kitchen, Luke looked in the fridge for something to eat. "I know he is probably starving," I thought to myself.

I asked, "Luke, how do you feel about McDonald's?" Excitedly, he looked up at me and said, "I love McDonald's!"

"Great, then we will stop and get you something to eat on the way to my house. But first, put this shirt on!"

"Okay," he said with excitement.

We exited the house, and Luke said, "One second, I need to lock up." He pulled a key from his sock, locked the door, and we left. As I backed out of the driveway, I looked at Luke sitting in the backseat from my rearview mirror. I glanced at myself and asked, "Naomi, what in the world have you gotten yourself into?"

* * *

Typically, I don't sleep well when Kinney is away. But that first night, I slept like a rock, which I chalked up to being so emotionally exhausted from the previous day's events. "I better check on this boy," I thought.

I headed to the guest room where Luke was sleeping. I peeked into the room to find him in a deep slumber. He looked sweet and innocent lying there. "He spent a week alone doing God knows what, and the mental toll of his mom not coming home for a week probably scared him half to death." There was so much to unpack with this kid and his family. I returned to my bedroom and looked at my phone. "No phone calls from Valley Spring in the night—that's a relief," I thought. I called the hospital to see how Dixie was doing but could not reach anyone at the nurse's station.

Again, I didn't panic because I'm sure I would hear from them if Dixie...

At some point today, I will go to the hospital to check on her. But we should probably go back to the house and gather a few more of his things just in case.

After a shower and a few minutes with my executive assistant, Drew Colby, or DC as I call him, we moved a few things off my schedule.

"Dr. Martinez, not to overstep, but you seem uncharacteristically distracted. Is there anything I can help with?" I appreciated DC's sentiment but was slightly offended by his spot-on observation.

"That's very thoughtful, DC. Just shift the meetings like I've asked. Essential ones can go tomorrow in the a.m.; others need to be shifted to next week if possible."

DC replied skeptically, "Okay...I'm on it." Before we concluded, DC said, "Oh, last thing really quick, Dean Jamison called and mentioned needing to align with you before the conference this week. Should I schedule a follow-up for you?"

The fact that Garrett Jamison, Dean of the College, called was surprising, but it reminded me of the long email I hadn't responded to a couple of days ago. During my undergrad years, Dean Garrett Jamison was just graduate assistant, Gary. Our familiarity dated back at least 15 years. He was intelligent, handsome, and confident. His ease made him a student favorite in front of the classroom.

In contrast, he always seemed tentative, even nervous, in any one-on-one interaction with me (like when we'd meet to review a grade or discuss my research methods papers). Over the years, though, he leveraged his smarts and demeanor to network and politick his way to one of the top jobs at Middleton State. I'm not saying he wasn't qualified or capable, but he'd have had a much more challenging path had he not won the birth lottery *and* been easy on the eyes.

I didn't quite understand how to interpret it back then, but in retrospect, he probably liked me. I was already sold on Kinney, but Garrett Jamison might have had a shot in a different life. My parents would have had a fit, though. "Naomi with a white boyfriend from Middleton?" They would have had something to say. As I'd grown in influence and visibility, Garrett had always been a positive and encouraging presence, hence my participation in his upcoming conference for the school.

"No, DC, I'll make a point to call him back later today. Thanks for your support."

"Sure thing, Dr. Martinez. Take care," DC said.

I was ready to get going. I returned to the guest bedroom to wake Luke up. He was still sleeping peacefully with his head under the blanket, balled up into a fetal position. I tapped his shoulder gently and whispered his name to avoid startling him. He turned over, popped his head from the covers, and smiled.

"Well, good morning! Did you sleep okay?" He nodded and stretched a bit.

"Good. So, here's the deal. I need you to shower and get dressed. Everything you need is already in the bathroom." I pointed across the room so he'd know which bathroom to use. I had already laid out some clothes for him to wear and a toothbrush for him to use. I keep spare toiletries around the house because my nephew stays with us sometimes. He and Luke seemed to be around the same size, maybe the same age, which reminded me how little I knew about this kid.

"When you finish, we'll eat some breakfast. Then, we'll go back to your house to pick up some of your things."

He nodded enthusiastically. "After that, you and I are going to see your mom! How does that sound?"

His mood suddenly changed. "I guess so," Luke replied with a shrug. He climbed out of the bed and headed toward the bathroom. I wasn't sure how to interpret his reaction. I straightened up the bed he'd slept in and turned on the television to make the room feel a little livelier for him.

After 30 seconds, Luke exited the bathroom wearing the same oversized basketball shorts and tee shirt he'd worn yesterday. From the looks of it, he hadn't bothered to shower or put on the clothes I laid out for him.

"I'm hungry," he said. I looked down at him and decided to let it go. We headed downstairs and into the kitchen. I opened the pantry, where he had several choices of cereal to choose from. As he ate, I thought about how many outfits I would need to pick up for him but reminded myself that he wouldn't be here that long. "It's just a matter of time before one of his family members takes him in. They'll probably be more upset than I was about Charlotte leaving him unattended for days. I can't wait to see that blow up in her face."

I wished I could figure out who they were and where they were... but I barely knew Dixie.

Watching Luke finish his cereal, I thought, "Poor little guy. And he's got the nerve to be super cute too." I shook my head. Luke had the innocent look you'd expect from a kid his age, which reminded me to ask, "Luke, how old are you?" He lowered the bowl from his fat cheeks, wiped his mouth with the back of his hand, and said, "I'm eight. I was seven for a while, but then I had my birthday. So, I'm eight now."

"Okay, that makes perfect sense," I chuckled. Despite all the chaos that seemed to be swirling around him, he had a sweet quality.

We left on foot and headed to Luke's house. It would have been a fifteen to twenty-minute drive this time of day, but we could easily cut across the park and get there at the same time if we walked. There were a few clouds, and I thought it might rain. "Wouldn't be the worst thing considering how hot and dry it's been," I thought. We exited the subdivision, crossed the street, and started our mid-morning journey. It seemed like an excellent time to ask him a few more questions.

"So, Luke, you told me you were eight. When is your birthday?

"May 15th"

"Oh, so not long ago. Did you have a cool party?"

"No, my mom said she couldn't because she just got her job, and we couldn't have any parties yet."

"Yeah, some jobs are like that, I suppose."

We ventured further along. His familiarity with the wooded paths off the main walkways surprised me. "We can go this way," Luke yelled.

"No, let's stay on the main path," I said.

"But this way is faster. I always go this way."

"Well, I'm going to go this way, and I'll probably get something sweet from the Coffee Cart."

On the Oakmont side of the park, vendors set up along the main path, and the Coffee Cart is a local fixture. I thought the idea of a snack might lure him back to me, and I was right.

As he rejoined me, another pair of midmorning walkers passed by us. I made eye contact and smiled a cordial greeting in their direction. The couple noticed him, glanced at me, and looked back at him with concern, never reciprocating my politeness.

I noticed, obviously, but I didn't give it pause.

I resumed my Q&A session with the recently turned eight-year-old.

"So, I know a little bit about your mom. Where is your dad?"

Luke raised his hands, palms up, and said, "I don't know."

"Do you see him at all?" I asked.

"Nope," he replied in an emotionless tone. I decided to let the dad topic rest. He didn't appear to care much, and I'd already been briefed when Dixie and I met that fateful day a week or so ago.

"Who else do you have in your family? Do you have aunts or uncles that ever come around to visit?"

"Yeah, kinda, I do. I have Uncle Kyle and Uncle Lawson, but I hardly ever see him. Uncle Kyle comes over and yells at Mom about dumb stuff."

"What about Aunt Charlotte? Do you know her?"

"Oh yeah. I forgot about her cause I hate her... and my stupid cousin, Jennifer. They suck."

"Whoa, Luke, you are too little and handsome to have a mouth like that! And *hate*... hate is a strong word. Why would you say that?"

He explained how Charlotte and Kyle kicked them out of their aunt's house. He expressed how it made him feel. It was fascinating to hear him describe the event. When he finished, I asked if he remembered the last time he'd seen them.

"It's been a long time. Aunt Charlotte was over here a week ago, and Mom went with her. But they just never came back.

I shook my head and patted him on the shoulder. "Well, you're going to see her today. That should make you feel a lot better, right?"

"I guess," he shrugged.

Once he caught wind of the Coffee Cart, he sprinted ahead of me with excitement. Again, I noted how calm he was about his mother. It reminded me of our exchange in the bedroom. My radar began to blip again. Beyond all the other family dysfunction I was picking up on, I now felt that there might be something truly amiss between Luke and Dixie.

CHAPTER 10

When we arrived at Luke's house, there was a ton of commotion. People were walking in and out of the house. There was a giant dumpster not far from the driveway. It looked like someone was simultaneously moving and holding a garage sale, given the amount of furniture sitting in the yard and people rummaging around.

Luke said, "Hey, that's my Uncle Kyle..." Then, he asked mysteriously, "Why's *he* here?"

"Good question," I thought.

Kyle was a middle-aged guy, about six feet tall, with a noticeable beer belly and blonde mullet that reminded me of that movie Joe Dirt. Uncle Kyle looked like we caught him with his hand in the cookie jar as we got closer.

Luke, with a skeptical frown on his face, said, "Hey, Uncle Kyle..."

Uncle Kyle looked at him and never spoke. He loaded a box into the cab of his truck and then stood there looking at me with an oddly mystified expression. Uncle Kyle was so busy staring at me that he couldn't greet his nephew. I thought, "Is it just me, or do these folks *love* to stare?!?"

The moment reminded me of a conversation with one of my closest friends, Ferrin. She would have referred to Kyle's behavior as a 'micro-aggression.' "You might think they're trying to intimidate you, but when some white people stare at us with that look of confused wonder, various, often stereotypical assumptions are buffering in their minds. And they will stare at you until they've applied the assumption they think best explains your presence within their situational space. Fight or flight? Freeze or appease? Trust me when I tell you, they'll snap out of it the second you *stare back*."

Which is precisely what I did. After locking eyes with Uncle Kyle for a few seconds, he looked away without saying a word. Whether he was stymied by my arrival with Luke or trying to make me feel unwelcome, he set a tense and discomforting stage for our impromptu visit.

I looked down and saw that Luke was already headed into the house. I took a few fast strides up the porch and through the door to catch up with him. I entered behind him, and to my surprise, the place was damn near empty!

Around the corner came a tall, broad-shouldered young woman with multicolored hair. She was wearing a floral maxi dress and a seasonably inappropriate white cardigan. After the silent and uncomfortable staring match with Uncle Kyle, I was prepared for the worst, but she was cordial and introduced herself.

"Hello, my name is Jennifer, I'm Loretta's cousin... and you are?" she asked with her hand extended.

"Naomi Martinez," I replied. As we shook hands, I could tell she knew my name. I assumed she spoke with her mom, Charlotte. I could feel the tension among the few other people moving about the house. I was good at 'reading rooms' because I did it for a living. Judging by the reactions I observed from their body language and facial expressions, things were all good until Luke and I showed up. And I certainly wasn't the person they were expecting.

I was about to explain that Luke and I were there to pick up a few of his things. But, before I could, Luke came out of his room frantically. "I can't find my stuff! Where'd all my stuff go?" He was in a state of disbelief. Jennifer had a look of guilt on her face, and her posture immediately became defensive. I knew something wasn't right, and I told Luke to show me his room.

Luke's room was completely empty! No bed, no clothes on the floor, no toys. Just empty.

I was shocked. I asked Jennifer, "Where are Luke's things?"

She looked at me with her arms crossed and, in a hushed tone, said, "I dunno. I guess they're probably outside."

Now, when she said outside, I was under the impression that his belongings were packed up in a box, sitting outside to be loaded onto Kyle's truck or something. Then, it dawned on me, "...if they are clearing out the house, then Dixie... must have passed away... Oh no, Luke has no idea," I thought.

My adrenaline spiked, and I walked out the door, but I saw no sign of a small child's things being packed up for a move.

I asked Jennifer, "What's going on? Where are Luke's clothes and whatnot?" Maybe it was just me, but it felt like everyone started to move faster. That's when Jennifer pointed towards the dumpster.

I looked at the dumpster, then back at the young woman. "His clothes... in the dumpster?" I looked at her and the other people moving about the porch and yard with dismay and frustration. "Why? Why would his things be in the dumpster!?!"

Jennifer looked around and replied, "You'll have to ask my mom about all that." Her attitude went from defensive to ambivalent. And that's when I became even more incensed about the entire situation.

I paused. I squinted and stepped towards her, slowly and

rhetorically asking, "Well... Your mom isn't here right now, is she?" Before she could answer me flippantly, I raised my voice and said, "That's why I'm asking you!"

My voice and the look on my face must have conveyed my disgust. Seeing this dying woman's family raid her home without regard was beyond anything I expected to witness. Jennifer stood there, looking back at me with resentment and a hint of fear.

I looked into the house as Luke continued to sulk about his missing things. I looked back at everyone in the yard and asked, "Did Dixie pass away?" That was the only reason these people would have to come over and remove her things from the house, but it still wouldn't have made it OK to throw Luke's belongings in the dumpster.

Jennifer rolled her eyes and shook her head no.

I couldn't hide how stunned I was. It was as if someone had punched me in the chest. I rubbed my forehead, and after a second, things began to crystalize in my mind. I declared, "If that's the case, then legally, none of you should be here taking or selling anything out of her house until the estate is settled. Does Dixie know that you are all here cleaning her out? This is a crime, and I'll call the police right now." I pulled out my cell phone and started pointing it around like I was filming. People began to hunch their shoulders and hide their faces from view.

Jennifer was in over her head at this point. Fearing that people might leave, she replied loudly, "Look, my mom knows we are here. She arranged for us to clean the place out, and they all decided who would get what and what we would sell and whatnot, so..."

"Wait a minute." I interrupted. "You all decided what you all would get and what you all would sell?!? She's still alive, Jennifer! And you guys are here, making decisions about her and Luke's belongings?!? All of this belongs to Luke, whom I know you left alone for a week. I have a good mind to call the police right now." A few sprinkles of rain began to fall from the sky.

Jennifer stood there with an increasingly nervous look on her face. I raised my voice to embarrass them a bit more. "Yeah, that's right! Did you know this little boy was left alone while his mother was in the hospital fighting for her life?!?" I moved closer to Jennifer to make my point even clearer. "Here you all are taking whatever you want from this house, but who's taking him!?"

Luke had made his way from the house into the driveway. He'd found a half-inflated basketball and pointlessly shot it toward the basket opposite the driveway. The scene wrenched my heart as I pointed in his direction to cement my point.

"That wasn't a rhetorical question! I'm assuming one of you is taking Luke too. You're taking everything else that matters to him and his mom."

The silence was deafening. My 'outburst' may have seemed theatrical, but I was upset. "In all my years, I have never met people this awful! I'm calling the cops."

The onlookers may have been family, neighbors, or complete strangers. I didn't know or care, but they started whispering and rushing toward their cars rather than the house. "Good, they should be fleeing the crime scene," I thought. The sprinkles were building to a light shower, and I thought, "Lord, walking over here was a mistake. Please have a car nearby to pick us up." I opened my phone to ping a ride-share. "

"Six minutes away?! At this time of day? Amen! Get us up out of here..."

I looked up from my phone, which had a few raindrops, to find Luke still playing on his basketball goal—the only thing they didn't have a chance to throw away. Jennifer must have thought she was off the hook because of the rain. She stormed off towards the house while texting on her phone, face red with embarrassment.

"Hey, Jen, we're not done!" I said it loud enough for her to look back before her pace quickened.

"Is this bitch *running* from me?" I shook my head and calmly approached the house.

Jennifer was inside with Kyle and two other people I didn't recognize. With my phone in hand, still gesturing like I might call the authorities, I said, "Look, I'm not playing with you all. What are you planning to do about Luke? Are you taking him, Jen? What about you, Kyle?"

Kyle damn near hid behind Jennifer when I said his name. Meanwhile, the tight-end-sized niece shrugged her shoulders. "It's Jenn-uh-furr, and Dixie put YOU down as the person she wanted him to be with, so that's that."

I said, "You are his family; we both know he'd be better off with his family during this difficult time!" I questioned the truth as the words fell from my lips, but still...

Jennifer responded, "Well, I know my mom won't be taking him, and I'm pretty sure the rest of our family feels the same way," as she held her phone up to show me a text message screen as if it displayed an official decree or something.

I was speechless, staring at her. I could not believe this exchange. I thought, "...not one of these Beverly Hillbilly impersonators said a single word to Luke; they're his flesh and blood... He's seven (or eight). I don't know. He's an innocent, little kid. Their kid!"

I was floored. I looked back outside at Luke. He didn't show any interest in his cousin or uncle either. "What the hell is happening here? What's up with this family?"

My phone buzzed in my hand and displayed a notification that our ride-share had arrived. I gave them each a disapproving scowl as I made my way to the door. At that point, it was raining much harder. Luke had made his way to the porch as I exited the house. He stood beside me, and I put my arm around him.

I turned to them from the porch and said, "You haven't heard the last of this—none of you, and you ought to be ashamed of yourselves." I locked eyes with them to make my disgust unmistakably clear.

"Hey, buddy, our ride is here." He turned away from the front door and saw the new electric sedan sitting silently and conspicuously in front of this bogus yard sale.

"No way! That's your car! I heard about those in school. They don't need gas."

Yep, that's right," I patted him on the back.

"I'm glad we're not walking back!"

"Nope, not this time. Come on." We hurried down the driveway through the rain and climbed into the back seats of the sleek sports car. As we drove off, I saw Jennifer and Kyle watching us and exchanging words. I could only imagine what they were saying.

After a few minutes of riding, Luke spoke.

"Naomi?"

"Yes, Luke?"

"Why was our stuff outside in the rain?... Why did they throw all my stuff in that dumpster?" He looked at me for an explanation, but I didn't have one appropriate for his young ears off the top of my head.

"I don't know, sweetie, but I'll tell your mom, and she'll get to the bottom of it."

He sunk low in his seat before uttering, "I don't have anything now." He leaned his wet, little head on my arm. All I could do was look at him, hold him close, and sigh.

The driver overheard our exchange. She gave me a concerned but sympathetic look through the rearview mirror and shifted her eyes back to the road. We arrived at the house, and as we exited the smart car, the driver signaled goodbye to me with a hand over her heart and an approving nod.

I returned a polite and appreciative smile, but inside, I was fuming at what just happened and what it meant for Luke. And Dixie. And most importantly, me.

CHAPTER 11

*O*nce we returned home, I sent Luke to the boy's room. He turned on the game system and played while I planned the next steps. "Luke, get out of those wet clothes and put on the stuff I left for you earlier."

"Okay!" he said. The fiasco at his house now had to be addressed, as does Luke's caregiving situation. Things were getting messier and messier, and I still hadn't spoken to Dixie! I checked my email and sent a couple of follow-ups to keep the lights on work-wise. There was a message with an update about the conference, but it was too long for me to digest. The family drama I'd been involuntarily drawn into was diverting all of my focus.

At the same moment, a text arrived from Kinney with pictures of himself, and Dad buried in the sand, presumably by Nick, Noel, and Kinsey, who were posed triumphantly around them. The photo gave me the nudge I needed to resolve this situation so I could join them as scheduled. I left my desk and entered the boy's room to check on our little houseguest. When I entered, Luke was dressed in my nephew's outfit (the one I left for him originally). "Looking good, Luke."

"Thanks," he said, without looking up from the game, a reaction I'm all too familiar with from all the boys, Kinney included.

"I have to run a few errands and then go to the hospital to check on your mother. You can either come with me, or I can drop you off at the athletic club."

"Yes! The club!" He tossed the controller on the floor and went to put on his shoes. "Luke, hold up. You need to put things back the way you found them." He huffed in response, looked back at where he was sitting, and realized what I meant. I watched as he frowned, returned to the TV stand, wrapped the controller up, and pushed the chair back to the desk. "Okay, good. Now, come with me."

I grabbed a spare Nike backpack from the past school year and walked downstairs into the pantry. "Here, let's get you a few snacks and some drinks so you can keep your energy up at the gym!" Looking through the pantry again, I could tell he was amazed by how much food was in there. It's not like we were prepared for the apocalypse or anything, but it was a timely reminder that Luke and Dixie didn't come from much. Thanks to Charlotte and Jennifer, they don't have much now. But his reaction...I wondered how excessive 'plenty' may look to someone with so 'little.' I told Luke, "We don't take anything for granted because we never know when things will happen. We have to ensure we have enough...just in case."

He nodded and replied, "Save it for a rainy day." I nodded, "Exactly, like today!"

I remember in church as a child hearing the pastor say, "To whom much is given, much is expected." As he put the backpack over his shoulders, I could feel how much it meant to him to go into that athletic club with new clothes and a new (to him) backpack. As Luke and I drove to the athletic club, I said, "I'm glad my nephew's outfit fits you. Do you know what size shoe you wear?"

He answered, "These are a five, but I need a five-and-a-half 'cause I'm getting bigger and older now." I smiled as he continued, but I heard all I needed to hear. Those funky little shoes are getting replaced ASAP, but first things first. I pulled in front of the gym entrance, put the hazards on, and escorted him in.

I asked the front desk staff to sign him in under our membership as a guest. One of the attendants recognized him.

"Oh hey, Luke!"

"Hi," Luke politely responded.

The attendant looked back and forth at Luke and me with confusion, then asked, "Where's your mom?"

I knew what the attendant was insinuating, so I interjected before Luke could answer. "His mom is under the weather, and I'm looking after him today. Make sure he has access to the game room and indoor pool."

Luke looked at me and said, "Whoa, you have indoor pool access?! I never get to go in there."

The front desk attendant looked at my club membership status and quickly corrected himself. "Of course, Dr. Martinez...I. Just. Didn't. Know," he stuttered while looking at us with embarrassed curiosity. I returned a noticeable expression of disapproval to let him know that I caught him red-handed. I left it at that so things wouldn't become any more awkward than they had already become.

"Okay, Luke. Have fun, and I'll be back in a few hours. If you need to reach me, they have my number." I looked back at the attendant with a cue to confirm.

"Um, yes. That's right, Dr. Martinez, we sure do. We'll take good care of him. Thanks."

I returned to the SUV and exited the parking lot onto Main Street. I sat at the light, deciding whether to turn right or left. I recalled all that had happened earlier that day. With Charlotte making all of the decisions for the family, including an impromptu fire sale of Dixie and Luke's things, I began to believe what Dixie suggested to me when we first became acquainted. Nobody in her family circle had their best interest at heart. Shaking my head, I thought, "I need more answers... Dixie is the only person that can provide them. If I don't act fast, I might miss the chance altogether."

I decided that my other errands could wait. Instead of turning right, I left and drove back to Valley Spring Hospital.

* * *

WHEN I ARRIVED at the hospital, two nurses left her room, exchanging pleasantries with the surprisingly spry patient. "Hi, Dixie! Look at you lighting up the room!" I said with an excited tone. Her eyes lit up, and she flashed her big smile. "Hello, lady!" she said. Seeing her alert and talkative felt good because she wasn't doing well when I last saw her. She urged me to scoot a chair over to her bed so I could sit at her bedside.

"I'm sorry, Naomi."

"For what?" I asked.

"I'm sorry I didn't tell you I was putting your name down as my emergency contact, but I didn't know what to do."

"I think you knew *exactly* what you were doing", I thought. Out loud, I replied, "Yeah, that was a big surprise... I dropped him off at the athletic club a bit ago, but he's stayed with me at our house. He's safe and sound," I reassured her.

"I can't thank you enough. I mean that."

I continued our conversation. "So, tell me, how are you feeling?"

"Right now, I'm okay. They keep me pumped with all these pain meds between treatments." She giggled a bit before an awkward silence filled the air between us.

"I'm supposed to go home tomorrow with hospice. They are trying to see if they can deliver a hospital bed and whatnot."

In my head, I thought, "That's all she's going to come home to because her family just cleaned her out — literally."

"Dixie," I said. "I know you've been medicated heavily and may not remember, but have you spoken to any of your family today? "

"No... Not today. Why do you ask?" she replied.

I had never been the type of person to mince words, and I'd tell you what was on my mind even if it got me into trouble, per se. But this was the second time in as many minutes that I thought better of coming out with the truth. Given her condition and the first-hand context I had with her kinfolk, I decided that empathy and restraint would be the better course of action - at least for now. Seeing how she'd be home tomorrow, the band-aid would be ripped off soon enough - why be the messenger? She'll know that her so-called family, friends, and neighbors did her wrong and be able to confront them as she sees fit.

But I had to be honest with myself at that moment, too. "What about me?" Outside of Kinney and a random cab driver, no one had shown me compassion or understanding for the position I'd been involuntarily thrust into. Inside, I shouted, "This wasn't the kind of me-time I had in mind a few days ago!" I was entitled to that emotion but had to get out of my feelings and prioritize. I thought, "The clock is ticking, and unfortunately, time isn't on her side, or mine for that matter." I knew I needed her to help locate the right family member or resources to make long-term arrangements for Luke. She seemed alert and coherent, but that could change at any moment. We needed to have this conversation, even at the risk of making this sick woman feel worse.

"Dixie, you know all of this is a shock to me."

She nodded.

"You said you weren't well, but now I know it's far more serious.

She nodded again, but this time, she hung her head slightly. I could tell where this was headed. I grabbed her hand gently. "It's okay. It's okay. But I feel like you should tell me everything. What's going on with you? You never shared the truth of what you're facing with me."

"I know, and I'm sorry for that," she said, her eyes closing and opening slowly. "...I have some rare form of cancer. It came back to get me. Did I tell you I had breast cancer?"

"Yes, of course." I nodded. "I remember *you* telling me that, but I didn't even know your real name then..." She shook her head regrettably, but I encouraged her to go on. "You told me that you'd beaten it. And it seemed like you were fine - physically."

"Yeah, well, I first discovered the cancer when I was pregnant with Luke."

Still holding hands, I gasped, and our grips tightened. "They wanted me to start treatment after the first trimester ended, but I declined. I didn't want all that poison going through my system with him in there."

My mind quickly raced to consider other substances she may have consumed that potentially affected Luke in utero, but I didn't dwell on it long. She continued, "Once he was born, I underwent radiation, which was mostly successful. I had this healthy baby, kept my hair, and left that deadbeat monster Cash as soon as possible!" She laughed, and I smiled, but I was far from amused by anything she'd just shared.

She continued, "The cancer had been in remission for what felt like forever. I was feeling fine until recently. I know I should have been doing more regular follow-ups, but it was hard to keep up with the protocol... I had been unemployed, but you know about all that."

She sighed, "Now, they're saying the cancer has metastasized, and it's not good." She paused momentarily before adding, "Naomi, this is the end of the road for me. I knew it as soon as I had to call Charlotte."

She rolled her eyes at the mention of her sister-cousin, and tears poured down her cheeks.

"I hate this for you," I said.

Dixie released my hand to grab a tissue. Sobbing, she explained, "I knew something was wrong. I started having the same symptoms as last time. I had this awful feeling when I came to the doctor this time. I knew I wouldn't be so lucky. And now here we are."

I took a deep breath before I responded. "Dixie, there's no good time for this, but we have a lot of ground to cover with this emergency contact thing and the fact that you are just leaving Luke in my care instead of your people."

Dixie reacted apologetically, "I know, I know I should have... Wait, is he here?! I haven't seen him in days. Weeks! I asked Charlotte..." Her panic was surprising, but I remembered how medicated she'd been.

"Relax, sweetheart. Like I said earlier, he's been with me for a couple of days now. I took him to the gym, and he's just fine. We'll get to all that, but..." I paused.

She urged me to continue. I grimaced and said, "Dixie, with everything you have going on, I hate to be the messenger."

"No, please, what is it?" Dixie asked.

"Luke and I went to your place earlier today to grab a few things for his stay at my house."

"Sure, was something wrong? Did something happen?"

In my mind, I responded, "Oh, you mean, aside from your son being left unattended for days on end by his cousin-aunt or whatever?" Aloud, however, I was much more gentle. I informed Dixie that her niece Jennifer was there with Kyle and several others, moving things out of her home.

"It was like a garage sale or something. Several people were there there. People like your brother, sorry, cousin Kyle, were loading things into their cars. Some of your things had been tossed into a dumpster. And apparently, that's where all of

Luke's things wound up. Dixie, I couldn't believe it. I raised my voice and threatened to call the police, then it started raining, and people started leaving - like they'd been busted. I was so taken by it... I.. Well, I had to ask them if you were still..."

I couldn't finish the sentence. I just shook my head and looked away from her.

There was silence.

It was obvious that she pictured everything I reported to her as vividly as if she were there. She didn't respond verbally. I looked back up to see an expression on Dixie's face I could only describe as numb. I held and rubbed her hand again. I thought how awful and sickening it had to be to hear what happened. But I was right to tell her. I thought again, "She just needs to make it home. Alive." And just like that, she was off into a medication-induced slumber.

I sat there with her as she slept for a while to soothe her and maybe to comfort myself a bit. I hated that our talk exhausted her, but I blamed more of that on the morphine than the messenger. Plus, that was only the tip of the iceberg. This whole mess was of titanic proportions.

As I quietly rose from the chair and began walking out of the room, the charge nurse came in to take her vitals, waking Dixie up. "Are you trying to sneak out on me?" she asked warmly.

"No." I laughed. "But you need your rest," I replied. She nodded but wanted to continue our conversation.

"So, I know you went by the house... Jennifer and Kyle were there, you said?"

I didn't replay everything but did confirm what she seemed to remember—that Luke saw his Uncle Kyle at her house and that I had a run-in with Jennifer. "I hate that bi..." Dixie said. She noticed my surprised yet approving look and continued, "...sorry you had to meet my family like this. My family are the last people I want around me in this situation, and I'd NEVER let them handle any of my personal affairs. My sister Charlotte and her daughter Jennifer are just awful people." She adjusted her body to an upright position as the nurse continued tending to her machines and ports.

I didn't know what to say, so I listened until she asked, "So, they threw some of my baby's stuff in the garbage, huh?" I nodded regrettably.

"I'm not surprised. They've never liked him."

"That just baffles me. How do you not *like* an eight-year-old kid?!" I asked.

She replied, "I don't know. It has everything to do with how they feel about me, though — none of my family has ever wanted anything to do with us. It's always been him and me, against all odds, as they say."

The charge nurse gave me a look to suggest that Dixie would be unconscious soon and to wish her a good night. It was evident that soon meant a minute or two, if not less, as Dixie's eyes began to flutter. I told her not to worry about it and encouraged her to rest easy. "Luke is fine, and this will be fine too. We'll talk more tomorrow at your house 'cause you'll be home." She smiled, her eyes closed, and she was fast asleep.

Although I knew this could be the last time I saw her alive, I didn't feel that chat would be our last. I had many more questions, but I'd have to settle for the little information I gathered while she was coherent this evening. Whether intuition or hope, I left the hospital believing she'd live beyond her doctors' and her family's expectations.

CHAPTER 12

On the way back across town, I still had time to stop by Berkshire Square and buy Luke a few pairs of shoes, socks, and other essentials I had hoped to get from his house. As I recalled his shoe size, I thought about the whirlwind that had taken place over the last 48 hours.

"I know I'm her emergency contact, but no one mentioned medical power of attorney. That must be Charlotte, too. Why would Charlotte have her sent to an empty house for hospice? Just despicable."

The more I pondered it, the worse I felt about everything. The situation, the trip, my schedule, the speaking event coming up… I didn't know how I'd gotten myself into any of this. But I knew I had to figure a way out.

Shopping isn't something I do as often as I'd like, and I certainly don't shop for myself often enough. But as I looked for Luke's new things, the many Naomi's in my mind had gathered again, and the court was in session.

"As a matter of fact," Naomi said, "I'm shopping for this woman's boy I don't even know. I thought I was going to have some me-time...It's been absolute chaos since Kinney and the kids left!"

Bougie Naomi replied, "Hmph. You don't know her family, but from the little bit you've experienced, they are not the type of people we should have anything to do with."

Pragmatic Naomi said, "Luke might need to go to foster care if we can't find a suitable family member to take him." Cynical, alpha-female Naomi said, "Are you kidding?! You got into this dysfunctional family mess the minute you trusted 'good old heart' over there and visited these people a couple of weeks ago, duh!"

In unison, all the Naomi's turned to me with disapproval, "Good-hearted Naomi strikes again," I guess.

"Cash, check, or charge? Ma'am...?" The question took me off guard and snapped me back to the moment. I realized I was staring at the clerk and holding up the checkout line.

"Sorry, here you go," I said, handing her my credit card. "Would you like to round up and donate to..." I didn't give her a chance to finish.

"Absolutely." It was a subtle reminder to the jury that I, Chief Justice Naomi Goodheart, remained firmly in charge.

As I collected my bags and headed to the next store, my phone rang. It was another one of my best friends, Gio.

Gio and I have known each other since the fourth grade when his family moved to Middleton from Yuma, Arizona. He lived directly across the street from my family, so we spent much time together. After his parents divorced, he lived with his mother and grandma. Gio would visit his Dad in his 'fancy condo' a couple of weekends a month. Things were tense between him and his father for as long as I can remember. He would return from those weekends and tell me how mean his father would be. He always said he wouldn't have to see him again one day.

Meanwhile, Gio's mom was strictly business, and her business was fashion. She was a designer making and selling clothes from their house to people in their community. Morning, noon, or night, you could count on 'Mama G' to be photo shoot-ready! Wigs, make-up, gowns, robes... slippers with heels! Come to think of it, I don't think she ever owned a pair of sneakers. She had every color of high heels you can imagine. Her closet was like a different universe; we loved spending time there.

Mama G was stern about manners, behaving in school, finishing chores, and being responsible for ourselves. But she was also very caring and gentle, especially about Gio being comfortable in his skin. He spent a lot of time emulating his mother. As we got older, the visits to his dad's place became far less frequent, and Gio became more unapologetically himself and happier than ever.

Mama G's consignment business had gotten too big for their house, and she expanded over the years. By the time I was in college, they'd opened several boutiques called 'House of De'Leon,' and Gio was an essential part of that growth. Several years ago, a famous model wore one of Mama G's designs during New York Fashion Week, and the family business became a household name among celebrities, trendsetters, and fashionistas. Now, you can find House of De'Leon boutiques in Las Vegas, Miami, and New York City. Gio occasionally works out of the original shop in Braxton Square but spends most of the year in more cosmopolitan places than Middleton.

"Nay!!" Gio's voice has the enthusiasm of an old friend and the disciplinary tone of his mom. "¿Dónde está, mama?!? Where have you been? Why have I not heard from you?"

My grin widened, and I replied, "Gio, I'm so sorry for not calling you. Would you believe I'm at Braxton shopping! I'll have to stop by the boutique. But look...there has been some crazy stuff going on! I need you to send an SOS to the girls for me."

"An SOS... for real?!? Oh no, things must be really off the chain," Gio exclaimed.

SOS is the distress signal for our friend group, and when one of us sends that text, it means it's time for an emergency, in-person meeting among the four of us. My closest friends and an ample supply of wine and whiskey at our earliest convenience.

"Yes, to say the least," I said with a chuckle of despair.

"Well, are you okay?" Gio asked.

"Yes, for the most part...I think. I need help making sense of the last couple of days," and I gave Gio the abridged version of all that had transpired.

"Ay, dios mio, Nay-Nay... This is like something off TV, girl. I can't...," he said with sorrow and regret. I realized I hadn't heard that nickname in so long. It was the nickname he gave me back in elementary school. I always thought it was because 'nay' is the first syllable of my name, but he claims it has something to do with 'all in favor, say I,' and me being the one most likely to vote 'nay.' He's a fool for that.

"Should I be scared? Gimme a heads up 'cause I'm too old for bad surprises," he asked. Did I forget to mention that Gio was dramatic as hell? His concern was warm and genuine, as always - and I appreciated it more than he knew.

"Scared...well, no. But...please, just round up the troops, Gio."

"Okay, love. I'm all over it. Watch your texts, but I will call you with the location and time. You're all heart... ever since we were kids. Hang in there, mi amor."

"Love you too. Bye."

It was a 10-minute drive from the mall to the gym, where Luke played for the last few hours. I called the front desk and informed them that I was on my way. "No problem, Dr. Martinez. He's in the activity room, so we'll get him ready for you." I looked forward to showing him his new shoes and outfits. Luke buckled up in the back seat when I pulled up at the gym. We headed home, where I'd made us something to eat, and watched television before bedtime.

"Luke, I have some news for you." He looked up from an old tablet I'd given him to play with. "Your Mom is coming home from the hospital tomorrow!" To my surprise, his reaction was flat and uninterested. "Hm... okay." He looked back down at the table and continued playing his game.

* * *

DIXIE HAD BEEN DISCHARGED from the hospital to be home with family for hospice care. Charlotte has been there helping, which couldn't be helpful for Dixie's comfort. Luke and I made our way over to see her. I thought I would finally get to pin down who in her extended family she thought would be best to keep Luke as we prepare for the inevitable.

Since taking Luke home with me, I'd learned a few things about the eight-year-old over the last three days. I learned that Luke wasn't a fan of healthy, home-cooked meals. He would prefer to eat sweets and junk food all day and night. I also noticed he did not have a hygiene routine, such as showering in the morning or brushing his teeth before bed. He would have worn the same clothes if I hadn't made him bathe and change into one of the outfits I purchased for him. Otherwise, Luke appeared to be an easy-going kid, but there was something I couldn't put my finger on. He was easily distracted but could focus on his interests, like video games, cartoons, and music. He wasn't afraid to be out at night. But really, he didn't seem bothered by much, including everything happening around him. Most of all, he didn't seem concerned with his mother dying. It wasn't my priority to figure it out, though. I'm focused on ensuring this kid spends as much time as possible with his mother. I sadly thought, "The memories will have to last him the rest of his life."

Luke and I pulled up at their house. Upon arrival, there was only one car in the driveway. I thought there would be several cars and a house full of visitors, but there was no such fanfare for her return.

Luke jumped out of the car and ran toward the house. When I approached the doorway, Luke stood there looking up at Charlotte. She stood there like a beefeater, guarding the entrance from an intruder. I saw what she was doing, blocking Luke from walking further into the house. Luke looked up at me, waiting for me to say something to this big bully keeping him out of his own home. "What's going on, Charlotte?!

"Loretta is sleeping right now. Maybe you two should come back later."

"Later?!" I whispered, "There might not be a later Charlotte. This is HIS house and HIS mother. Now, I'm sure she will want to see her son. Please. Move."

Charlotte reluctantly backed away from the door as we carefully squeezed past her bulky frame. As I nudged Luke forward, I looked her in the eyes, thinking, "Who the hell do you think you are, telling him to come back later, knowing his mother can die at any time?" I wanted her to feel my disdain as we went to Dixie's room.

When we entered, Dixie was lying on her side facing the door. Despite the frailty of her appearance, her eyes opened. She smiled and extended her hand slowly toward Luke. After glancing at his mother momentarily, he looked down and stood there with a cute but emotionless expression.

I could only imagine what was going through his mind, considering it had only been the two of them together. He is going to feel so all alone when she passes. I am truly sad for him, and he sure as hell can't stay with Charlotte the Barbarian (who I could hear slurping her fountain drink in the other room).

With a sense of dread, I seriously thought, "What's going to happen to this poor boy?" It had been only a few seconds, but they seemed like hours, and he hadn't looked up or moved. "Poor baby...he must be afraid, but maybe he's in shock," I pondered.

This was a lot for me, so I felt I could empathize with his paralysis. As he remained motionless, eyes fixed on the floor, I gently placed my hand on his shoulder. I whispered, "Luke, look up. It's your mom. She needs you to be a big boy right now. Go and hold her hand." He looked up at me, finally raising his head, and locked eyes with Dixie. She began to smile. He stepped a bit closer to his mother's bed. I was relieved and congratulated myself for saying what he needed to hear at such a critical moment. I thought Luke would take his mother's hand, but he didn't.

"What are you leaving me when you die?"

It was as if a record scratched in my mind. "Did this boy just say what I think he said?" Dixie was staring at him in disbelief (just like me). I looked at her out of shock, then looked down at him. Luke was staring back at Dixie and appeared to be growing impatient, waiting for her answer. It dawned on me that this kid was dead serious, and from the hurt and embarrassment I could see in Dixie's eyes, she realized it, too.

I couldn't believe what I was seeing. I grabbed Luke by his shoulders, turned him around, and kneeled to put the fear of God in him. "Boy, don't you EVER speak to your mother like that! EVER!" Luke was shocked. Just as I hadn't seen this side of his personality, he hadn't experienced this side of mine.

His body flinched, and he looked at me with a snarl of anger. He saw the same intent in my face as his aunt, and his demeanor became more apologetic.

"Okay," he muttered.

"Now, tell her you're sorry," I ordered. Luke reluctantly leaned toward the bed, embraced his mom, and apologized. Luke looked back at me and asked, "Can I go outside?" I glanced at Dixie, who was holding back her tears. She gestured to let him go, so I nodded, and he rushed out of the room.

All I could do was shake my head and hold my chest. It was so heartbreaking. "How could he? What kind of eight-year-old asks a question like that?! Christ. Maybe the apple doesn't fall from the tree," I thought, considering what I'd heard about his dad. I started to get my mind around it. His apology was forced and remorseless, and he couldn't escape her fast enough. He knew his mother was seriously ill weeks ago and went on like it was nothing. He stayed home by himself for days, like it was nothing...

Dixie's voice interrupted my mental process. "He has always been a handful," Dixie said.

"A handful? Please," I said to myself. Luke might be something else entirely. I deferred to my training, breathed, and held Dixie's hand. "Kids...they don't know how to process stress on this level. This whole situation is overwhelming for him. That...that wasn't him. That's not how he feels about you," I said. There was so much shame and embarrassment in her face.

So much so that she looked away from me and said, "No, it's okay. I left him here alone. I've made so many mistakes. He hates me just like everybody else."

I frowned and tried to convince her otherwise, but I've seen her family and how low they regard her. "Dixie, there's no good time for this but the present," I said. "We have to make long-term arrangements for your son, and I'm...well... I'm not the solution, dear."

She shook her head no. I replied, "Dixie, there has to be someone you know and trust, closer to you and your family... here or someplace else who can take him."

She just shook her head, tears streaming down her face. "Dixie, you don't know me. We talked once; I'm a stranger. You don't just leave your child with a stranger from your..." I stopped short of saying deathbed, but she inferred precisely where I was going.

"You're not a stranger to me, Naomi! I know your heart. I feel your spirit. I knew you the moment I met you! I don't have anyone else to turn to. You've met my sisters and brothers… they hate me and Luke, all because of me. That's my fault. I'm so sorry for everything I put you through.

But even if I did have someone else to call, they wouldn't be YOU, Naomi."

The acknowledgment was necessary. The apology was appreciated, and the compliment was humbling. Her whole situation, however, was bleak. "Dixie, I appreciate all that. I do. If the shoe were on the other foot…you'd better understand how odd this situation is for me. I'm trying to do the right thing here, but… you have all this family right here in town. They were just here ransacking the place the day before yesterday." Dixie wiped her eyes and laughed, "Right, so you know what I mean! They're horrible rednecks, Naomi. And Luke? Luke would be ruined with them."

I couldn't argue with her, but my reluctance remained intact. Dixie said, "When I first met you, I thought Luke would be fine with you, and I believe you could straighten him out."

She may have thought she was on a roll, but I was far from flattered. Mentally, I replied, "What? This isn't the old days when you hired dark-skinned help to raise your pale-faced children. I'm not interested in 'straightening your son out.'" An inner voice kicked in. "Honestly, Naomi, what vibe are you giving off that says, 'When you pass on, leave your kid with me?' I nodded in my mind. "I need to correct that impression."

I suppose the expression on my face said it all. Dixie had just made the best case she could. While I felt deeply for her and Luke's situation, my uncertainty was too much to mitigate. The toll of this heart-to-heart was taxing on both of us, but in her depleted state, exhaustion was my excuse to leave.

"Dixie," I said, "I will let you get some rest. Is it okay if I come back later?"

"Yes," she said, eyes closed but with a loving smile. "It would be wonderful if you did."

I whispered, "Okay," as I pulled the covers over her and walked out of her room. "Love you, Naomi."

I paused mid-stride and looked back over my shoulder. "You too, Dixie."

As I approached the front door, the house was oddly silent. There was no sign of Charlotte the Barbarian or Luke, and her car was gone. I thought, "I need to separate myself from this situation for a while. Maybe she took Luke somewhere. But what if she didn't? She should have let Dixie know she was leaving. He should have let somebody know he was leaving. Ugh, these folks are entirely too much for me."

As I made my way toward my car in a bit of a frustrated panic, I had to check myself. Pragmatic Naomi said, "Relax. Dixie is back home; this time, she has a qualified hospice nurse to keep watch."

Alpha Naomi chimed in, "I know that's right! So, he'll be back when Luke is done sky-walking or night-crawling. And, they'll be home to sit his little butt down."

A few seconds later, I received a text message. "We're set to meet. Vicenza at 7 pm," complete with bottle, martini, and girlfriend emojis.

"Ahh, Gio." I thought with a smile. He'd sent the SOS I asked for. My loyal squad and I getting together at one of our favorite spots later provided a much-needed escape from my current plight.

"I responded, "LOL, looking forward to it." I needed to be around some positivity and trusted advice, mainly because Kinney wasn't here. Gio's text and a few moments with my friends would be just what the doctor ordered. Literally.

CHAPTER 13

I arrived at the restaurant. Gio and Ferrin were already seated. Ferrin is another close friend whom we met sophomore year of high school. She's always had a boss vibe—very smart and persuasive. Her talent is knowing how to motivate and rally people. She was the president of several clubs and organizations throughout high school and continued to develop her activist chops throughout college. After working in executive roles most of her career, she opened her own consultancy helping grassroots and nonprofit political organizations across the country lead protests for human rights, environmental rights, women's rights, voting rights, and social justice.

Ferrin is a revolutionary at heart. I remember some posters on her wall when we were kids. The Tommy Smith and John Carlos poster from the 1968 Olympics with their fists raised. The 'Vote for Shirley Chisholm' poster too. She's always been passionate about fairness and equity. We were not surprised by her success, and I was interested in hearing her perspective.

I greeted my friends enthusiastically as I approached, "Hello, hello!" I made my way to Ferrin first with cheek kisses and an embrace. "Ferrin, it's so good to see you. I've missed you. I'm so glad you could make it."

She replied, "Oh, Naomi! Girl, it's been too long. You haven't aged a day. I had to 'heed the call,'" referring to Gio's 911 message.

I walked around the table to Gio and greeted him similarly. The fourth member of our party hadn't arrived, but knowing her, it wasn't a shock. "So, where is Mrs. Tinsley?" I asked sarcastically.

"Girl, please! Tinsley is always late. She's on 'colored people's time' more than me!" Ferrin said. Gio and I giggled, and we all settled into our seats.

Ferrin wasn't exaggerating. Even for those who love her, Tinsley would be aptly described as 'hair on fire.' It's not a dig at her, but it's her personality—theatrical, over the top, someone who can go from zero to sixty like a fast car. And, like a fast car, she's a bit more liable to crash occasionally.

Still, she's ambitious, determined, and unafraid to speak her mind, which are qualities I certainly appreciate and admire. She can be difficult, however. I diagnosed her as being 'addicted to busy,' as evidenced by the two cell phones (and paired Bluetooth devices) she always carries, her over-reliance on daily checklists (and compulsive need to complete them), her inability to take time off or detach from work when she does. Gosh, even the way she 'power walks' everywhere.

Last month, during a quasi-therapy session (aka drinks at her executive loft downtown), I told her, "Tins, it's like you have to be everywhere at once, and you can't be anywhere long enough. It must be exhausting. And to go as hard as you do every day. It's not sustainable."

"You might be right, Nay," Tinsley replied. "...but that's what these are for!" showing me a few pills she had inside a Guerlain compact stashed inside her Hermes bag.

"Girl, Benzos in a Birkin bag? Tinsley, your life is a reality show right now." We laughed. I continued, "As a doctor, I wouldn't advise taking those with..."

"What, this?" Tinsley pointed to her half-empty wine glass. "Xanax pairs perfectly with Miraval!" She finished off her sparkling rose with a look of guilty satisfaction. I just shook my head.

Regardless, Tinsley, or Tins as I sometimes call her, is one of my best friends. If you want to have fun, she's the one you call. She has been that way since our college days.

Sometimes, we had too much fun and paid the price in the form of hangovers. But we never missed our early morning classes, no matter how badly we felt. We were both overachievers, but our motivations were very different, as time would reveal.

Since then, Tinsley has become a highly sought-after event planner (which makes sense given her energy and checklist orientation). She's thrown upscale events for high-profile businesspeople, political figures, and celebrities. She was also responsible for planning my elaborate fairy-tale wedding to Kinney.

"Eeee, look who it is!" Gio quietly exclaimed as he first noticed Tinsley enter the dining area. We all watched with entertained anticipation as Tinsley power-walked through the restaurant, talking authoritatively on the phone and approaching our table. She waved at us, which was partially a greeting and partially a signal to hold on as she finished her conversation, but Gio had already wrapped her up in a wide hug, basically saying,

"Time's up, boo-boo."

She made her way around the table kissing cheeks.

"Okay, make it work, and I will be in touch after dinner," Tinsley said into the flickering device in her ear as she sat down at the table. "Okay, what did I miss?"

"Nothing yet, we've been waiting for you," Gio answered. Ferrin added, "You are not nearly as late as last time. I'm impressed."

"Don't start, Ferrin. I just sat down!" Tinsley said with a smirk. If looks could kill, Ferrin would be on trial for murder. "So, what will we be drinking, ladies?" she asked rhetorically while signaling the nearest waiter over. "We'll have a bottle of the Kosta...and the Hyde de Villaine."

"Damn, Tincup, you got the whole wine list memorized?!" Ferrin said.

"Honey, it's been one of those days. And, maybe I do, but that's beside the point." We all laughed. I did say she was the life of the party.

"But what is really going on, Naomi?" Tinsley asked.

I took a breath as the waiter returned with our bottles. As he filled my glass with Pinot Noir, I started recapping the last few days with my closest friends.

"So, you guys know some kids from the neighborhood are always playing in my backyard?" Everyone nodded their heads. "Well, one of them came over to play before the boys came home two weeks ago. As he went to play, he nonchalantly told me his mother was ill. He actually said, 'She's sick.'" Gio immediately put his hands on his heart with a sad face, while Ferrin and Tinsley leaned in and continued to listen.

"His mother came by our house looking for him later that evening. This was the first time I ever saw this woman. I hadn't put two and two together though. I told her he wasn't there, only to find him and Nick chatting it up in the near-dark backyard."

They all looked as if this might be a major plot twist, and Tinsley's brows began to furl with skepticism.

I continued, "That night, I just could not sleep. I tossed and turned thinking about this sick woman and this little boy. Total strangers...I can't explain what it was, but it was clearly heavy on my heart. Maybe I was thinking, "what if I were in that situation?"

All my friends were nodding their understanding as I took in the looks of concern on each of their faces.

"It gets worse," I told them. Tinsley refilled her glass with more wine, and now Ferrin and Gio are holding their glasses out for Tinsley to fill theirs.

"So, you all know that I pray."

Gio responded, "Yes, yes. And pray for the waiter too, please. Tinsley, I see you!" He whispered his scorn sarcastically as Tinsley objectified the male waiter with her thirsty stare.

Ferrin rolled her eyes at the playful duo then said, "Ahem... please, Naomi, go on."

"I went through my prayer, meditation and breathing routines but couldn't shake the feeling. So, I asked Nick where they lived and walked on over."

"Wait, you did what?!" Ferrin exclaimed quietly.

"Sweetheart, I know you are an award-winning psychiatrist and whatnot, but that's doing the most. You always want to help..."

Gio interrupted Ferrin mid-sentence.

"Ferrin, easy mama! Maybe she was supposed to go over there...You know, God's will," he said.

Neither Tinsley nor Ferrin looked convinced and proceeded to sip more wine. "Guys, let me finish," I said. "She had a lovely personality, but she was sad. She told me about her dysfunctional family, and we had a good conversation, but that was the end. She wasn't well, but she wasn't dying either. A week or so later, right after Kinney and the kids left for Belize, I got a call from the hospital telling me that I had been listed as some random lady's emergency contact.

"Wait, did I miss something?" Gio said, looking around the table.

"How sick is this lady that she would put you down as an

emergency contact, and emergency contact for what?" Ferrin asked.

"She's terminally ill," I said. As soon as the words left my lips, the table gasped. "Oh my God, Nay!" Gio said.

Ferrin responded, "Oh, hell no, Naomi. Let me guess. This woman must be psycho?"

Tinsley barked, "What is that supposed to mean? I don't even know why you'd go there right now."

"She's different alright," I said.

"Nope, nope, um um," Ferrin said, shaking her head. "I don't like it."

Gio added, "Yeah, I'm with Ferrin. Who would do that? She doesn't know you. Where is this woman's family?" In her signature, smart-aleck tone,

Tinsley retorted, "Humph, clearly not listed as the emergency contact."

Ferrin and Gio smirked in agreement, but didn't drift from the gravity of this news.

"Um, and that's still not all," I said.

Tinsley exclaimed "Geez-us Christ on the cross!" and threw her hands up before finishing the last of her wine. Gio and Ferrin shook their heads with amusement and embarrassment.

"She wants me to care for her son," I said.

"While she is sick?" Ferrin asked, with a disapproving look on her face.

"No," I said.

"After she passes away?!?" Gio said, with his hand over his mouth. I nodded my head yes. Tinsley looked at me and shook her head no.

"Honey, what are you going to do?" Gio asked with a concerned tone of voice.

"Tell her no!" Ferrin said. "I can empathize with her situation, but asking YOU to do something like this? Absolutely not."

"I agree with Ferrin on this one," Tinsley said. "There are so many variables to this situation...I'm not sure you are prepared to handle it."

In a stern voice, Ferrin said, "Fuck those variables, girl! You need to tell her ass no."

Gio said. "I don't know...I feel so sorry for the kid. Things must be horrible if she wants a complete stranger to take her son. There has to be more to this story because no one would do that...unless they didn't have a choice, right?"

I chimed, "I have no plans on keeping him. But I won't feel right if I don't try to find someone in that family willing to take him. But the family members I have met? They are not interested. Not one bit. Oh, and I forgot to mention, he was left home alone for about a week—all by himself. And he didn't even know his mom was in the hospital."

Gio gasped. The look on Ferrin's face made her appall clear. Tinsley looked mortified.

Breaking the silence and after a few more sips of wine, Tinsley asked, "Nay, how old is this kid?" "He just turned eight," I replied.

All three sighed and repeated, "Eight?!?" Everyone in earshot must have heard them.

Tinsley's reaction was over the top enough to attract attention from the other guests in the restaurant. The ladies (Gio included) gathered themselves, and there was another silent pause. Clearly, it was a lot to take in for all of us.

"Imagine living it," I thought as I poured myself another glass of wine and continued my story.

"So, the next day, I went to Dixie's house to grab some clothes for Luke."

"Wait, who is Luke?" Gio asked from the edge of his seat as if watching a movie. "Is that the kid's name?" "Yes, his name is Luke," I said.

"Aww, that's a cute name. I'm guessing his mom is Dixie?" Gio asked.

"Right, Dixie is Luke's mother, but hey didn't have her by that name when they called me originally. They only knew Loretta Wade; I'd never met anyone by that name."

"Oh, that's why you didn't know who the hell they were talking about!" Ferrin exclaimed. "This is too messy!" She took a big sip and said, "Okay, okay, so you went over to get this child some of his clothes?" I confirmed and went on.

"Right! So, he and I went to his house. It was like a garage sale when we got there, but her family members were just taking stuff. Clothes, furniture, boxes, and containers with who-knows-what inside. And anything they didn't want was going into a small dumpster." I paused and took a sip of wine. The emotions were un-ignorable.

"This woman's not even dead yet!" Tinsley said while motioning her head side to side in rebuke.

Nodding, I responded, "The sad part was that they didn't 'want' most of Luke's things."

They all looked confused momentarily, but I realized it was more discomfort than disbelief. I had to ensure they knew the full extent, so I continued.

"Yeah, you heard me. These so-called family members took this boy's belongings out of his room and threw them in the trash. So, no clothes, no shoes, no toys. Nothing. I gathered old clothes from around the house for him to wear."

They moaned in unison again. "Girl, enough is enough," Ferrin said, waving her hand. "Get out of this now before something bad happens!"

"Too late for that," quipped Tinsley.

Gio in his most persuasive voice said, "Naomi? Dr. Naomi Martinez, who I've known my whole life? You are a psychiatrist. You know this whole thing is mental. So, what are you going to do now?"

"I don't know exactly, but I'm not giving up on the family doing the right thing yet," I responded. "At least his mom is home, but she can pass anytime. Hell, she could have passed away while I'm sitting here talking to you guys."

Ferrin broke the silence, with a deep sense of concern and skepticism, "Naomi, what is Kinney saying about all of this?" "He knows some things, but I will fill him in on the rest tonight when he calls."

"This is unbelievable," Gio said. "I'm so sorry, Nay. But I know you will find someone to take him. Everyone has assholes in their family, but the whole family can't be that way.

Someone will come through and take this baby."

Tinsley huffed, "Humph, I disagree," looking at Gio like some naive child. "Family can be your worst nightmare. Trust me on that one." We all kind of smirked, knowing the messes Tinsley had been in. "But don't get me wrong, Nay. I do hope you find someone to take care of him."

Ferrin asked, "What can we do to help?"

"Just stand by. You know...I'm still wrapping my head around it all," I replied.

"Well, let us know when you need us. We got you." Ferrin said. Almost on cue, our server came over to check on us. Gio and Ferrin looked at each other like they might be claiming dibs on the unsuspecting young waiter.

Tinsley looked at them, and said, "Oh, I love the nerve from you guys! Like I'm the only thirsty thirty-something at this table." We all looked at each other and laughed out loud.

Their company and laughter helped lighten my mood. Ending these last several days on such serious notes has really strained me, so this was nice. We each went around the table to share the latest and greatest truths, or 'tea' since last we met. The cuisine was delicious, the laughter cathartic, and our time together was well spent.

We hugged and said our goodbyes, ending our time together on a high note. It would be a matter of minutes before I started thinking about Dixie and Luke again but getting them off my mind for a bit was the perfect medicine.

CHAPTER 14

$\mathcal{I}$ remember the following morning vividly. I slept in a bit later than my usual early start. The dinner, all that wine, and a brief check-in with Kinney had made it easier for me to get a decent night's rest. I made my coffee and put on the morning news before looking at my list of consultations for the day. With the speaking event approaching in just a few days, I knew I'd need time to refocus to get my speech and sync up with the organizers. I connected with DC, and we started with the day's calls.

After a couple of hours of sessions, my mind began drifting, and a feeling of anxiousness came over me. One of my inner voices said, "You know you don't have time for this right now. There's no telling what's happened at Dixie's while you're sitting here."

I asked DC to reschedule my remaining calls.

"I can, Dr. Martinez, but..." he said reluctantly, "I just want to remind you to connect with Dean Jamison. He called again, and his voicemail sounded rather urgent."

"Sure, DC. Just go ahead and call him back to find out what he needs. I have to get going." I knew I ended the call more abruptly than usual, but something told me to get over there, so I powered down the home office and headed over. I pulled up to Dixie's house a little more nervous than usual. Given she could go at any time, I didn't know what to expect. After speaking with my friends and Kinney yesterday, I felt ready to tell Dixie to make other arrangements for Luke. There was no sign of Charlotte's car, and Luke was playing basketball in front of the house.

"Hi, Luke," I said.

"Hi!" he replied as he continued to shoot the ball. "Is your mom asleep?"

"I don't know," he said. "Have you been inside?" I asked.

"No," he said, as he dribbled the basketball.

I stood there looking at Luke quizzically for a second.

"You haven't? So, did you leave with Charlotte yesterday?"

He replied nonchalantly, "Nope."

"Then where were you?" I asked.

"I went over to my friend's house."

"Luke," I said, "come here for a second." He shot the ball and huffed as he made his way over to me. I wanted him to look me in the eyes so I knew he was listening to what I was about to say.

"Luke, the next time you want to go to your friend's house, you must let ME know. You understand?"

"Okay," he nodded enthusiastically and hurriedly said, "K, can I go now?"

"Not yet. Come inside with me and let's say hi to your mom." I would have asked, but I feared his response after the last time.

Luke ran into the house and Dixie's room. "Hi, Mom," Luke said.

An upbeat and alert Dixie responded, "Hey Lukey-dookie, what's up with you!?" Seeing her with more positivity and energy than the day before was great. Of course, by energy and positivity, I mean sitting up in her bed with both eyes open.

As I looked at her interacting warmly with Luke. "Cancer is a bitch," I thought. All the resources we have in this world, and we still can't solve for this?" Despite my mental tangent, I was glad to see a normal interaction between them for once, and it gave me a bit of relief.

Dixie asked, "Luke, are you going back to Connor's house to hang out?" "Yep!" Luke replied in an excited tone.

"Okay, have fun," she said. I was glad someone knew where he was last night. I guessed that was their norm, but this wouldn't fly in my house.

As Luke exited the room, I asked Dixie, "How are you feeling today?"

"All things considered, today is a good day... at least, so far," she said calmly but cautiously.

"Oh, that's good to hear. So, has Charlotte or anyone else been over... any family?" "Well, Charlotte was...here yesterday, but nobody else...?"

Dixie paused and grimaced before continuing, "I'm not surprised, but I'll tell you what. I'm glad she's not here. I'm so pissed at her," Dixie said emphatically with a frown on her face.

"Did something happen?" I asked.

"Apparently, while I was in the hospital, Charlotte went through my purse." As soon as she said that, I knew this tale wouldn't have a happy ending. "She took my checkbook and went to the bank. Now, I'm not sure what web of lies she told them, but she somehow convinced the people at the bank to give her access to my account."

"Oh, don't tell me...," I sighed. "Don't tell me she robbed you, Dixie."

She hung her head and, with a quiet anger, said, "That bitch cleaned us out. She withdrew my money and closed the account...as if I'm already gone."

Floored by this news, I asked her, "How is that remotely possible? Did you have her listed on your account?"

Dixie exclaimed, "Absolutely not! I don't have much, but the little I did have...that was mine! Not hers to do whatever she wants with."

She began coughing from being so riled up. I hated seeing her demeanor go so dark quickly, but I couldn't blame her. She was infuriated, balling up her fists and pounding them on the bed. "She had no right to do that to me, Naomi."

"No. No, she absolutely didn't," I replied, but I wished I had more to offer her besides repeated apologies. We paused for a few seconds, and I broke the silence.

"I know what you can do. Call the bank. Tell them what happened, and they can get your money back. You know, fraud protection, identity theft, or something like that."

She didn't react to my suggestion, so I suspected there might be something more to the story she wasn't telling me. I asked, with concern, "Dixie, how did you find out? Were you out shopping before I got over here or something?"

She giggled a bit before continuing to tell me about this horrible situation.

"At some point after I got back home (and was conscious), I was looking through my purse. I noticed my wallet was missing. I didn't take the hospice staff for thieves; they've all been gracious and kind. So, I figured it was Charlotte and Jennifer—one of them anyway. I tried calling them and leaving messages, but Charlotte wasn't returning my calls. I still haven't heard back from her."

Dixie continued, "Honey, my spidey senses tingled like crazy, so I called the bank to check my account. The automated voice couldn't locate it with the information I was punching in. You know, like I didn't have an account open with them. I pressed zero until I got a real person. They said that according to my account notes or whatever, I showed up, withdrew all the money, and closed the account yesterday afternoon."

I shook my head in disbelief and started pacing the room

near Dixie's bed. "Girl, your sister-cousin-whatever stole your wallet, went to your bank with your card, ID, etc., pretended to be you, and took you of all your money?"

She nodded as if to suggest that there was no other reasonable explanation.

"Damn, Dix! Never mind calling the bank. You should be calling the police!" I said.

Dixie replied, "I know, right? She knew I planned to give that money to you...to help with Luke."

I stopped pacing the room and looked at her as if I had misheard her, but I could sense from her sorrow and defeat that I heard her correctly. She growled with a solemn look on her sunken face, "I won that money, not her."

Like I said, I knew there was something she wasn't telling me. "Won that money? You won some money, Dixie?" I asked. "Naomi. I actually won the lottery a couple of months back," she said, lifting her head to look at me.

I held my palms out and motioned for more detail. "The lottery...like, Powerball?" I said sheepishly.

Dixie smiled wide through her anger, "Ha! I wish! No, it was just a scratcher."

I don't know why I was so relieved to hear it was just a scratcher, but I was. In my head, I thought, "Nobody is scratching off a $150 million win—we'd have heard about that on the local news or something, and if Charlotte could withdraw it all in a day? Then it couldn't have been all that much."

Knowing the scale of the crime wasn't as epic as I thought helped me regain my composure, but still - it was a heinous act, especially for a family member to commit against a dying sibling.

Dixie continued, "I love to play scratch-offs. Whenever I grab a pack of smokes, I grab a few tickets. I might win five or ten dollars here and there. But, after all these years playing them, I finally won!"

"Wow, Dixie, that's so lucky. I've never met a lottery winner before."

Dixie posed her face like a wealthy debutante and in her best, wealthy debutante voice, said, "Well, now you have." She looked me up and down, and we both giggled.

She said, "I didn't win millions—it was a scratch-off. But, I won enough to move into this house and pay rent a few months in advance."

I nodded understandingly. "That money sounds like it was right on time! Sometimes, when one door closes, another one opens," I told her. I was, however surprised to hear her say that she was renting. I wasn't aware of any rental properties in this area, as most people here own their homes. I hadn't recalled ever seeing any rental signs in the yards, but maybe that was a growing trend on this side of the park.

I'm a little embarrassed to admit it, but I had wondered how Dixie could afford a home, even in this more accessible suburb of Middleton. As such, the lottery win explained much more than I would ever have asked or assumed.

It wasn't that important to me in the grand scheme of things. I know people wonder how Kinney and I can afford to live here, too. They're more likely to assume *we* won the lottery than Dixie and Luke and would probably prefer that explanation to the truth of our success— we earned it.

"Ugh, that thief Charlotte!" Dixie screamed out randomly, holding her head with a fist full of thinning hair in each hand.

"Why me?" she said, looking directly into my eyes.

"Everything in my life has been a disappointment. My family, my so-called friends, my health. I won the lotto but still have the worst luck."

With tears in her eyes, she muttered, "I can't even parent correctly, Naomi. I've disappointed Luke, my family, myself... and I know I've disappointed you, too."

I didn't know what to say or do for Dixie.

She'd had a very hard time.

She took a deep breath and wiped her tears for a moment. "Naomi?" Dixie said with an angry look. "Whatever you do, please do not let Cash take Luke. Please. We talked about him -- Luke's biological father. He can't have him," she implored.

"He is a two-bit hustling, drug-addicted woman beater. I hope he rots in hell. I have been running from that asshole for years, and I could never figure out how he would pop up out of nowhere and find me. My no-good family would tell him where Luke and I lived.

Time after time, he would show up looking for money or thinking I had something else he could swap for drugs. Then, he would beat the hell out of me and take whatever he could find." Dixie continued, but I had heard enough. Sure, I sympathized with her and felt bad for the hand life had dealt her, but this was the final straw. There is no way I'm keeping this child—I can't.

As Dixie went on, I fell deeper into my thoughts about all the ways this wouldn't work — the challenges that would arise for my family by bringing Luke into our home permanently. Dixie probably saw all these scenarios running through my mind before she added, "I can promise you this much: Cash will pop up after I die if he thinks he can benefit financially from having Luke. So please, be careful. He is very dangerous," she warned.

I thought, "This is too much, and this family is doing the utmost. The dysfunction, the disdain, the apathy, and now, the risk this supervillain named Cash poses. That was a nuance I didn't see coming. I imagined how Gio, Ferrin, and Tinsley would react to this bombshell. I thought about Kinney and I having to do something drastic to protect ourselves and our family from this dangerous criminal. I'd convinced myself at that moment that there was no scenario where taking Luke would be a good thing for us, no matter how good-hearted I wanted to be.

At the same time as I was going to tell her my decision was

final, we heard voices coming from the front of the house. Someone knocked on Dixie's bedroom door. A woman stuck her head in.

"Hi, Loretta," said the lady.

"Hello," Dixie replied.

" I'm with the hospice center. I'm one of the nurses that'll be taking care of you," she said with care and enthusiasm.

"Yes, I remember them saying someone new was coming to help me today," Dixie said.

Dixie's tone and demeanor flattened as she stared at Charlotte, who entered the room behind the nurse. She scowled at her sister-cousin and said, "Charlotte! I have been calling and texting you all day. Where the hell is my wallet, and what did you do at the bank, you snake?!"

Charlotte turned red and was visibly angered by Dixie's question. The nurse looked nervous as she was taking Dixie's vitals.

Knowing that Dixie had this well in hand, I said, "Okay, I need to run those couple of errands we talked about, but I will see you in a couple of hours."

"Of course, see you later, love," Dixie said with a smile from her bed while reaching out her hand to me. I grabbed her hand and smiled back, and my embrace let her know I would see her soon.

"Take care of her," I said to the nurse.

The nurse responded, "I sure will, ma'am."

From Charlotte's reaction, I knew she'd done all the things that Dixie had claimed. I looked Charlotte up and down with a judgmental frown as I stepped past her and exited the room. Charlotte looked back with anger, embarrassment, and perhaps a bit of fear that my errands might include calling the police to report her evil ass.

I rolled my eyes slightly as I walked toward the front door. "All. This. Mess. Every single moment with these folks has been a dumpster fire. But she very literally has no one else," I thought. I felt terrible for lying that I had errands to run. She knew that I didn't want to be there when they had it out over this bank situation. I had to admit that putting a slight fear of God in that big bully Charlotte on my way out the door was somewhat satisfying.

CHAPTER 15

*a*s I headed home, I reflected on what Charlotte did to Dixie and, by extension, to an innocent child (her nephew). What a horrible, greedy, despicable thing to do. I bet she thought Dixie wouldn't live this long, and she was trying to get all the money before anyone else in their family or Cash could claim it. I'd probably spent so many hours of the last four days shaking my head that my neck was sore.

It was a relief to pull up to the house after that. I'm not one to take what we have for granted, but I don't pinch myself about my life. I worked hard for it and deserve all the fine things I've earned. After all that with Dixie and Luke today, though, I looked around and said, "Thank you, Lord, for providing me sanctuary." I kicked off my pumps, poured myself a bourbon, and plopped on the couch in front of the TV with my tablet.

When I finished my drink, I was still unsettled. I'd need some additional firepower to achieve chill mode. I looked around. No noise, no children, no meetings. This was my moment - my window for the me-time I had hoped to get when Kinney and the kids left days ago. I smiled and went all the way in.

I went upstairs and took a bath.

I put on one of my favorite playlists and sat there for nearly an hour, sipping a second glass. This level of decompression was overdue. I oiled and wrapped my hair up, moisturized my skin, threw on my favorite sweats, and returned downstairs with a new, more relaxed attitude.

Remembering that I hadn't reached the grocery store, I ordered delivery and pulled up a new crime series I heard was 'now available on-demand.' I wasn't but a few minutes into the first episode when the doorbell rang. I knew my dinner delivery wouldn't be that fast, so I rolled my eyes and shook my head at the timing.

From the total home console on our coffee table, I could see that it was Luke and some women driving a red SUV, waiting for him in my driveway.

"What now?" I wondered as I went to the door.

"Hey, Luke! What's up, sweetie?"

He responded politely, "Hi. Can I stay at Connor's house tonight?"

"Well, I don't know…" I said with confusion. "I thought you were already at Connor's house?"

"I was, but I wanted to spend the night again. His mom said I could."

"Oh, okay," I said. "Well, I think you should ask your *mom*."

"I tried," Luke replied." "But, no one was answering the door. And you said to tell YOU when I'm going somewhere."

"Yep, I sure did. Good job!" I patted his shoulder and walked to the red SUV parked in my driveway. I greeted the woman sitting in the driver's seat.

"Hi!" she said in an overly enthusiastic tone while opening her car door. She came towards me with watering eyes and hugged me as tightly as possible. It caught me off guard, but I hugged her back as she began to sob.

"I'm so sorry. I'm just so moved by you," she said. I looked at her, not knowing what she was talking about.

"Moved?" I asked curiously.

"For taking in Luke and all. Connor and Luke have been friends since they were toddlers," she explained. "I'm just so sad to hear about Dixie. She's been through so much in her life, and now this." She reached into her car to grab a napkin, wiped her tears, and blew her nose.

"I'm Justine, by the way." She extended her hand to shake. I thought, "Eww, you just wiped your nose with that hand." I went through with the introduction, given how earnest she seemed.

"I'm Dr. Naomi Martinez. Pleased to meet you, Justine."

"Doctor? Well, that explains it! Your home is absolutely stunning!"

I thanked her politely, but after the backhanded compliment she'd just given me, interrupting my 'me-time,' incorrectly presuming that I'd be 'taking Luke in,' my body language quickly suggested that she should get to the point.

"Connor usually goes to his dad's every other weekend. I thought Luke could go with Connor — just with everything going on. You know, give him some familiar faces and friends to be around and take his mind off his mom's situation," she said. The comment struck me as odd, given the indifference I'd observed in Luke's reactions to his mother and her illness.

"Has Luke mentioned anything about any of that to you?" I asked emphatically.

"No, no. Nothing like that," Justine said. "Just that she was sick."

I looked around to see where Luke was. I could hear the faint sound of our trampoline in our backyard. Living up to my doctor title, I asked Justine, "Did he seem sad at all when he mentioned that she was sick?"

"Um, not really. I mean, I don't know. He was playing Pokémon or Mario with Connor, so I thought he was trying not to think about it. You know how little boys are? I'm sure he is since it's his mom, and he is the only child. But you know, kids..."

"Of course, Justine. That's probably it." I continued, "Look, things are still in the air, and this is a fluid situation. I emphasized that I wasn't his legal guardian, custodian, or anything like that. I'm just the person Dixie asked to help out."

"Oh. Sure. Ok. Right...," Justine seemed clearer after my explanation, and her tears had completely dried into her full, rosy cheeks.

"I'm okay with him going to your house tonight, but you should talk to Dixie about the weekend first thing tomorrow."

"Yep, say no more. Will do!" Justine said. "But, we were just at Luke's house. Seems weird that no one answered the door, though."

I hypothesized aloud, "He probably left his key in the house, and Dixie was probably resting through her last round of meds. Were there any cars in the driveway?" I asked.

"Well, just their pick-up," she said.

"Hmm, I was just thinking about the hospice nurse and their schedule. I would have expected them to be there, but who knows..." I trailed off. Justine nodded as we approached the bouncing boys in the backyard.

"'C'mon, let's go, guys!" I shouted.

He and Connor raced from the backyard and past us to Justine's SUV.

"Luke, you can spend the night over at Connor's house. I will let your mom know I gave you permission."

"Justine," I asked, "Could you please leave me your and Connor's dad's contact info? Just in case I need to pick Luke up early?"

Luke had a giant smile on his face as he and Connor climbed

into the backseat. Justine and I exchanged information, and she hugged me yet again.

"God bless you, Naomi," she said before getting in and backing out of our driveway.

I guess word of my generosity had spread across the community. I supposed there were worse conclusions that people could jump to, but I preferred privacy to popularity, especially in an unthinkable situation.

My dinner arrived as Justine, Luke, and Connor were leaving. I tried to settle back into my show and enjoy my meal, but I was too bothered by Luke not getting into his house to focus on either. For whatever reason, I just knew Charlotte was in there being spiteful and refusing to answer the door. I wrestled with myself because I told Dixie I would return, but I also knew she needed to rest. I think I'd just had enough of it all for one day.

"I'll go over first thing in the morning," I said aloud before finishing my food and two episodes of the new show I'd started binging.

The more I sat with my thoughts and emotions, the more I made peace with my decision: I will not keep Luke. "Worst case scenario, he can stay with Justine. That would be a much better solution— they've been friends forever," I thought.

At least, it sounded reasonable in my head. I understood and sympathized with their situation. I'd already gone above and beyond the call of duty for a good Samaritan. For me, though, someone who has only been in their life for a week or so at best... this wasn't a healthy situation to be so profoundly wrapped up in.

I had to be honest with myself, "Luke's life will change once his mother passes on, but I don't want that responsibility— raising him, charting his future... I've already put my ambitions behind me to be what my family requires. I've done more than my part in this already."

I moved from the living room and went upstairs to the

bedroom. I fell into the bed and moaned a deep, exasperated sigh before curling up and sinking into the mattress. My eyelids grew heavier by the second. The running back and forth with this situation had me physically exhausted, but I was mentally and emotionally drained, too. I was as conflicted as I've ever been about anything in my life. I acknowledged that Luke's life is already haphazard and destabilized, but he has no idea how much everything will change once his mother passes on. I found myself having another moment of radical candor as I dozed off.

"Do you really want the responsibility of raising him? Disciplining him? Helping him decide his future? And, dealing with the outcomes if and when things go sideways?"

"No. No, I don't. Final answer," I said, as if I were on a game show as both the host and the contestant. I drifted further into pre-sleep that night, confident in my decision, and committed to telling her first thing in the morning. I'd already spoken to Kinney and the kids for the night and would not let anyone disturb my sleep. So, I turned my phone off in a liberating act of space-making (and defiance).

* * *

MY MIND REMAINED unsettled despite laying comfortably between the sheets of our California King. I certainly wasn't 'awake,' but I wasn't fully asleep either. My eyes were closed, but I was *looking* into the darkness.

Consciously, I thought, "Just rest, Naomi. Rest." However, something very different was taking place. My surroundings began materializing through the darkness I was peering into moments ago. It was early morning, in the dusk-like moments before the rising sun peaks over the horizon. In the distance, snowcapped mountains and tall, evergreen trees became visible. I began to feel soft, moist grass beneath my bare feet. Neither warm nor cold, the dew drew my attention to the hazy atmosphere of this wide, quiet meadow. Through the light fog of what felt like an early autumn morning, I wondered, "Where is this? *What* is this? How...?"

I couldn't finish the question. A vague figure appeared in the distance. It was only a silhouette - something standing upright, but I wasn't sure what it was. All my mind allowed me to do at that moment was speak. "Hello? Hello, is someone there? Who's there!?" I asked.

My pulse quickened as the figure approached. My instinct was to move back and maintain a safe distance, but I couldn't summon the strength to do so. Something about this dream-like, semi-sleep state physically constrained my arms and legs. Unsure about where I was, how I'd gotten there, and why I couldn't move... I began to panic.

The mysterious figure held its position, like it could sense my fear, and stopped approaching so I wouldn't feel threatened.

As the sun's light began to overtake the early morning dusk, I could see the figure more clearly. It wasn't moving towards me anymore, but it appeared to be moving from side to side, perhaps spinning. The entire scene drew closer as I squinted to see the details before me. I focused more, and the scene drew closer still. The figure in the misty air resembled a person... not spinning, but dancing in circles as if it were celebrating. The movements were euphoric and appreciative like the figure had recently been liberated. I could literally sense the energy of the figure's joy — celebrating the gifts of touch, sound, and sight for the first time, all over again.

I could make out a few more details through the thinning haze. It was a feminine form wearing a long garment that flowed like a gown. Her dancing slowed to stop, and the shrouded form turned towards me. She resumed her approach in my direction, but instead of fear, I was overwhelmed with intrigue and curiosity. I wanted her to come closer, and she did.

She recognized me before I recognized her, but I knew

exactly who had joined me in this peaceful, ethereal meadow once that distinctive smile came into view.

Dixie. She looked so healthy. Vibrant, youthful, and carefree. Her skin was flawless, and the curls of her hair moved gently with the morning breeze. She truly looked amazing—renewed and refreshed. No sickness and no stress.

"Dixie, you look amazing! What are we doing here? Where is here?" I asked frenetically.

"Oh, Naomi! I *feel* amazing. I can't put it into words."

She spun around again, with her arms stretched from side to side. "I can't remember feeling this good in a long, long time... No. I've *never* felt like this. I could dance for days. I could run for miles. There's no pain, fatigue, or hunger here... do you feel it, too?" she asked excitedly.

I didn't. In fact, I was feeling something quite the opposite. Although I could appreciate her glee, I began to feel uneasy. The more I tried to feel what she had described, the more anxious and out of place I felt.

"Dixie, where are we? What are we doing here? I'm scared. I don't think I belong here." My unease was rapidly turning into despair. Dixie stopped dancing around, came toward me, and grabbed both my hands. Again, it felt as if she could feel my emotions change.

She gently whispered, "Thank you, Naomi, for helping us. You are such a wonderful person. I need you to know how much peace and hope you've brought into my life."

She looked into my eyes and smiled. She pulled me in and held me close. "I had to tell you how special you are before I go... and this time, I have to."

Dixie released my hands and backed away from me. The aperture around our picturesque moment widened slowly. And with it, Dixie's image moved further and further away from me into the pasture. Then, near the trees ahead of the distant, snowcapped mountains. Soon after, she was as far away as the figure I first saw and shouted at.

I wasn't sure what to think or believe. Still, the contradicting feelings that swirled inside me were unlike anything I'd experienced before — sorrow and joy, peril and gratitude, even motion and paralysis. As I tried to reconcile it all, I realized she'd just said, "Goodbye."

She looked back at me, smiled again, and waved.

I swear that I started running after her. I'm sure that I was yelling, "Wait, Dixie!" I kept running toward her, but I never got any closer. The mist grew denser. The dusk replaced the dawn. And after a few moments, I couldn't see her anymore. I couldn't sense the meadow or the mountains. Once again, I looked into the darkness of my eyelids and sensed the morning's sunlight was upon me in real life.

I awoke from my sleep, looking up at my bedroom ceiling. I watched the fan oscillate slowly above me. I sat up and looked around after rubbing my eyes. I pondered what I just experienced, and I attempted to go back. I closed my eyes and concentrated, trying to restore every detail from my memory, but no mountains, mist, or return trip.

I realized it was a dream. I knew it was a dream as I dreamed it. "But, Dixie just said goodbye to me in my sleep." The same sense of foreboding dread I felt came rushing back into my chest. "That has to be a sign," I reasoned. I needed to get to Dixie's house and tell her to make other arrangements for Luke because I wouldn't be keeping him. Evidently, I was running out of time.

I LAUNCHED out of bed in the same sweat I fell asleep in. I splashed water on my face, swished some mouthwash, and pulled my hair into a ponytail before getting in my car.

I noticed an unfamiliar vehicle in her driveway as I approached Dixie's house. When I visited their house, tense apprehension and stress would cascade through my entire body. "I don't want to be here. I didn't ask to be here, but I have to be here. I had to tell her my decision and get on with my day, week, and presentation... my trip to the kids. My life! I've gone above and beyond..."

I knocked on the door with authority, intending to wake whoever was on the other side. I waited for a few seconds, and there was no answer. Something told me to try the doorknob, and to my surprise, the door opened. I walked in slowly and headed toward Dixie's room. The house was still and quiet, with just a few beams of morning sunlight coming through the windows.

Unlike my knocking, I gently said, "Hello," as I tiptoed past Luke's room toward Dixie's.

"I'm back here." responded an unfamiliar female voice. "That's not Dixie or Charlotte," I thought, picking up my pace and looking into the room. I saw a woman in scrubs with a lanyard displaying an ID badge. She was in the room pulling linens off the bed and stuffing them into a transparent plastic bag.

"Hello," she said.

"Hi..." I responded as I looked around the room and hallway for any sign of Dixie's presence.

"Can I help you?" she asked politely.

"Where is Dixie?"

"I'm sorry, I don't know Dixie. I'm with the hospice center."

Annoyed, I clarified, "Dixie, the woman that lives here...the patient...um, Loretta Wade!?"

The woman stopped pulling down the bedding, and an uncomfortable look came over her round, wrinkled face. "Oh, I'm very sorry. From what I understand, the lady who lived here, Ms. Wade, died last night. I'm guessing you are a family member because you walked right in. You hadn't heard, I gather?" she asked, staring at me with concern.

I had no words. All I could do was stand there in shock. The hospice nurse paused and hung her head a bit. "I hate that you're finding out from me, of all people. I'm sorry for your loss." She paused respectfully as I continued to process. After a moment, she said, "Her sister, a lady named..."

"Charlotte..." I quipped scornfully.

"Yes, Charlotte. She told the hospice center it was okay to come on over and prepare the hospital bed and equipment for pickup."

I heard her, but my mind could only replay scenes from the dream sequence I had mere hours ago. "Last night, you said?"

"Yes, ma'am."

I could tell she felt for me and didn't relish being the bearer of bad news. I felt just as terrible, not just that she had to be the one to tell me but also that she'd barely departed before Charlotte was at work, erasing her memory.

"Do you have any more details about...?"

"No," she said gently. "I usually receive a call after the patient's body has been removed, and I come to get the equipment prepared for pickup."

I started to feel my lungs constrict and began having trouble breathing. "I'm sorry. I need to sit down for a second," I said.

The hospice worker politely exited the room. I sat down in the wooden chair next to Dixie's bed. I didn't expect her to go this soon. Just yesterday, she was active. She was coherent. She was here, right here, alive.

I started thinking about Luke and how he didn't see his mom yesterday. "Why didn't anyone answer the door?" My mind began to race, "Oh no, was she in here all alone during her final moments? The thought was mortifying, and my mind shifted again to Luke.

"He will never see her again and didn't get to say goodbye." Then, I pondered, "What am I supposed to do now?"

I sat there momentarily before gathering myself and exiting the room. I thanked the hospice nurse and started going out of the house to my car. Once the door shut, I lashed out.

"Damn it!" I said, hitting my steering wheel. "This is exactly what I was trying to avoid. I would talk to her today and tell her I couldn't keep Luke. Shit!" I shook my head for an eternity, thinking about what to do next.

I needed to text Kinney and tell him that Dixie had passed away and to call me. Afterward, I texted Ferrin, Gio, and Tinsley via SOS in our group chat to share the dire news. I needed to prepare to contact Connor's mom and dad and let them know that I'd pick Luke up sooner than expected. I knew she could die at any moment, but I thought we'd have at least one more day.

As I drove home, I couldn't help but repeat myself repeatedly, "What was I thinking?!"

I didn't want to get involved with this. I had no interest in putting my psychiatrist hat back on and examining Dixie, Luke, or their family, for that matter. "But, what choice did I have? What was I supposed to do with this kid? And this family? I don't know where any of them are. And even if I did, the ones I've met have no interest in this little boy. This is a total disaster," I thought.

I had to go and get my mind right.

My phone rang. Tinsley, the first of my friends, hit me back after the SOS text regarding Dixie's demise.

"Tinsley…" I answered solemnly.

"Oh my god, Naomi! I'm so sorry. I will be there as soon as I can. Hang in there, honey."

"I'm okay. You don't have to rush here, but I appreciate it."

"Nonsense, I will see you soon!"She hung up abruptly rather

than go back and forth about it. Tinsley has always been a person with difficulty taking no for an answer.

With the news settling in, I returned home and headed straight for the shower. Standing there, with water trickling down my face, I closed my eyes and began thinking about the dream repeatedly. The magnitude of it dawned on me. Dixie dancing in bliss, thanking me genuinely, in the middle of a peaceful nowhere. Then, she waved to me as she drifted away. It was so surreal and out-of-body. I wouldn't claim to be the most religious person, but as a God-fearing and prayerful person, I knew that 'dream' was too uncanny to be coincidental.

"That was actually her last night. She came to thank me... and say her final goodbye."

CHAPTER 16

J finished my shower and threw something on just in time to hear the tone of the doorbell. From the window, I saw the back half of Tinsley's white Mercedes parked in the drive.

Tinsley walked in, holding three cups and a bag. She puckered her lips and leaned in to kiss me on the cheek. "I thought you could use a soy chai latte, love," as she handed me one of the cups.

I prefer a medium roast but nodded, "Yes, you are a mind reader," and took a small sip. Tinsley and I sat in the foyer while she ate her gluten-free bagel stuffed with veggie cream cheese. She mixed her vanilla bean creme Frappuccino and her other cup of espresso.

"So, Nay, tell me what happened."

"Well, there is not much to tell. I was there yesterday speaking to her. This morning, she's gone. I never got a chance to tell her I wasn't taking her son."

"Oh, no!" she gasped. She put her hand on my shoulder and began to rub gently. "Why not? I thought that's what you planned on after we talked?" Tinsley asked, shaking her head in a caring but disapproving way.

"I was going to, but she was already distraught. She had just discovered that her sister-cousin emptied her bank account containing her remaining lottery money."

"Wait…" Tinsley said with surprise. "Lottery? What do you mean, lottery money? She won the lottery?" Tinsley's eyes lit up with excitement and a glimmer of hope that this story had some silver lining.

"Yes, that's what she said. But look, it was a scratch-off, not the Powerball." Tinsley hunched her shoulders, which made me giggle a bit.

"Well, still, how much did she win?" Tinsley asked.

I smiled but returned to the seriousness of the matter. "I don't know. Certainly not millions, and it wasn't much by the looks of it. It's irrelevant now because her cousin took it all. She went to the bank with Dixie's checkbook, ID, everything and withdrew every penny."

"What the hell!" Tinsley said, with a look of shock on her face. "She should sue her ass!" "How, Tinsley? She's dead." "Oh, yeah," Tinsley said. "Well, whoever takes the kid should look into that."

I continued, "Well, the hospice nurse was there simultaneously, and we both left the room so Dixie could have her moment with Charlotte. Dixie was getting frustrated; the sister-cousin looked crazy, and I just wasn't interested in being there for that." Tinsley just shook her head in disbelief and sadness.

I went on. "I was trying to let this woman know that I appreciated her faith in me, even though she doesn't know me.

But I didn't. I didn't tell her I could not be a part of this. And now, it's too damn late."

"No, it's not." Tinsley consoled. "Try to give him to anyone in his family and let them figure it out."

"I would, but I don't know where his family is or how to contact them.

Remember, these are the same adults, family members, who left him home alone for a week while his mom was in the fight of her life! These assholes couldn't care less about him, and it breaks my heart." I felt a few tears coming but fought them back.

Tinsley was fired up and put her arm around me. "Fuck that. Let's call Child Services and make this their problem, honey. That's what they're there for, right?"

I couldn't disagree with her on that one. Maybe she was right. Perhaps I should call Child Services and let them deal with all this. She could tell I was seriously pondering that idea when she added, "I don't feel good about this, Naomi. Get out now. These people will disrupt your life with their dysfunction. I know you have a soft spot. Especially for abused women and kids, and you are the best mom I know. Your parental instinct and care...look, I would be blessed to have you if I were in her shoes." That pushed my tears over the edge, but she went on. "These people are trouble, Nay."

She continued, "Honestly, you can't possibly know everything about this kid, this family, and where the hell is the "daddy"? Were they ever on Maury?!"

I laughed and wiped my eyes. "Tins, that's a whole different chapter."

Tinsley rolled her eyes and said, "Holy Hell, can we move into the living room for this part, please? I need to get comfortable...and we will need more than coffee for this! You got some

OJ?"

I poured a pair of tall pineapple mimosas with a splash of Grey Goose for some added kick (at 10:15 a.m., mind you). I told her all there was to share about Cash, including the apparent danger he posed to Dixie and Luke in the past.

"Another dangerous ass, deadbeat dad. For God's sake, if you don't make that call, I will," she said.

"Speaking of calls, I need to call Justine." "Who is that?" Tinsley asked.

"That's where Luke is right now. He spent the weekend with his friend."

I began shaking my head, an all too familiar involuntary reaction whenever I think of Luke. "I wish one of his family members would step up and at least be the person who tells him about his mom." I knew as I said it that no such thing would happen. "Shit, I'm the only person who knows where he is, and I'm the one who let him go. Argh!"

"Tinsley, finish your drink. We need to head back to Dixie's house and see if anyone is there."

"Say less! I'm ready." Tins chugged the rest of her Mimosa while I looked at her. "Really?" I teased with a smile.

I guess I was feeling hopeful. With Dixie out of her misery and all her money and belongings divided up, perhaps the family would come to their senses and be willing to take in their nephew. "I'm sure someone will be there," Tinsley said.

"We'll see. I'm texting Justine to bring Luke home when he wakes up. It's going to be a challenging day for him."

* * *

As we pulled up to Dixie's house, a man was loading a small box into the trunk of a late-model truck. "Hello," I said, walking toward the man slowly.

"Hi," he replied.

"My name is Naomi Martinez."

"Oh yeah, the doctor," the man said. I was surprised he knew, but he continued before I could ask. "I'm Lawson. My sister asked you to look after my nephew, right?"

Lawson. I remembered hearing the name. He looked

different from the other family members I had met over the past few days. He wasn't here with the rest of them stealing things while Dixie was in the hospital, but he's here now, which didn't sit much better with me. However, he seemed more pleasant, welcoming even.

There was no resemblance, so I deduced that he was Dixie's brother and Charlotte's cousin. "Ugh," I thought. "At least he's dressed like he has a job." To his credit, he didn't have that rural, seed-and-feed vibe I picked up from the rest of Dixie's relatives. Most importantly, he didn't seem taken aback by my skin color. Maybe he (unlike his wicked witch sister and niece) had time to digest the news that I was black. Whatever the case, he was considerably warmer and more personable than the rest.

He sat the box down and extended his hand, which I firmly shook as Tinsley looked on with judgmental skepticism. Lawson glanced over my shoulder to see my reinforcement, and a slight smile came over his face. "I take it you met the rest of the family?"

"Yes," I replied. "Your name hasn't come up in our recent chats, though."

Lawson chuckled, "Ha, not surprising. I'm adopted. My sister told you Kyle and Charlotte are our cousins, right?"

"She did," I said.

"Well, I'm sure you can tell I'm older than Loretta. After our mom passed, I was sent back to my biological mother. She had her issues, too, but rest her soul; she'd gotten herself clean and whatnot and put distance between herself and the rest of them. So, I never came around much." He paused before finishing his sentence, "...unless it was a funeral."

I looked Lawson in his eyes and said, "Listen, I'm going to be 100 percent transparent about this situation. I didn't *know* your sister. I had one single, solitary conversation with her two weeks ago. The next time I heard from her, more than a week passed, and the hospital informed me that Loretta put my name and number down as her emergency contact."

Lawson's face was stoic. I expected more of a reaction, but I continued with emphasis. "Lawson, I didn't even know your sister's real name until a few days ago." The wrinkles in his forehead grew more profound, and his face shaped into a concerned frown.

"Okay, he's putting two and two together now," I thought. I continued, "She told me she wanted me to keep Luke and raise him." "Like one of your own," he said, with a deep sadness in his voice. I nodded. "I'm sorry, Lawson, but I won't be able to do that."

Lawson's facial expression suddenly changed. "I'm so rude, let's go inside. I have a couple of other things to round up," he said as we walked into Dixie's home.

"So, Dr. Martinez, you didn't even know her, huh?" He asked. "That's just it, Lawson. I didn't. At least not long enough or well enough. I mean, I only learned her real name a few days ago. I had no idea who Loretta Wade was, so I thought it was a mistake when they called me two times in twenty minutes. I had only met her once--before she was in the hospital." "Yeah, I get it," he said.

As Lawson responded, Tinsley continued looking around the house with an icky expression, as if touching something inside might cause her skin to break out.

Lawson chuckled and shook his head.

"What's so funny?" Tinsley said, with her hands on her hips.

"Forgive me, ma'am. I'm not laughing at you; I'm not laughing at all. I can't believe the situation is all." Tinsley rolled her eyes even more as he continued. "My sister always made terrible decisions that affected everyone else but her. I'm sorry she dragged you into this, but I can't say that I'm surprised."

I jumped to the point, "So, you understand then. When Luke

gets home from his friend's sleepover, he can go with you, and your family can work out the details."

Tinsley nodded vigorously from the corner of the nearly empty room we were standing in.

"Oh no, wait a minute, ma'am. That... well, that *ain't* happening, Doc. Not a snowball's chance," he said, as his eyes widened. He started walking toward a couple of Rubbermaid bins, sitting across the room and moving faster as if ready to make a break.

"We... I can't take Luke."

"Hold up! Why the hell not? He's YOUR nephew!" Tinsley said.

I echoed, "Lawson, I don't understand. You are his family, and he'll be abandoned! What is it with you all? Why is it that none of you want this child? His mother is dead, his father is absent, and none of you will step up. He needs to be with family right now, and you know that as well as I do!"

With tubs in hand, Lawson said, "Look, Doc, there are clearly things that you just don't know."

"No shit, Sherlock! This is your chance to explain them," said Tinsley." Lawson dropped the tubs, clearly frustrated and wanting out of this escalating situation with Tinsley and me.

"I'll be frank with you," he said, looking directly into my eyes. "There's no way I'm taking that one anywhere in hell. And NO ONE else in the family will either. See, Loretta knew that..." He shook his head with an energy equal to anger and regret.

Tinsley and I looked at one another in disbelief and wondered, "What could an eight-year-old have done so awful that no one would care for him?!"

Lawson read our faces and continued, "That seems strange to you. I mean, it's a crazy thing to have to say. But Luke... that kid always has some real god-damned issues."

As Lawson explained, my mind replayed all the moments...

the ones when I wondered what sort of kid Luke was. Yes, there were red flags. I mean, what eight-year-old is outside of the house after ten p.m. unattended...regularly? I thought of how he informed me of his mother's illness in the first place. As calm and unaffected as he could be. Then, of course, how he reacted when his mother told him she was dying.

The "told you so" look on Tinsley's face broke my concentration. I tuned back into Lawson's voice.

"Maybe it was her lifestyle that...I'm sorry, you know... that made him the way he is."

"Are you fucking kidding me?!" Tinsley busted out. "He's. Eight. Years. Old!" she said, pausing between every word for emphasis.

"Exactly!" I added, which hyped Tins up even more. "Yeah, Uncle Lawson," she said sarcastically. "What has he done? Tortured and maimed animals?!? Kindergarten menace, terrorizing playgrounds across Valley Spring?! What the actual fu..!"

"Tinsley, that's enough," I said, turning to Lawson, expecting some answer.

Lawson rubbed his head, picked up the tubs, and headed full stride to the front door. "I'm not sure, but I can't do it. His mom was screwed up, and his dad is a screw up too. He can take him if I can find out where he is or get information on his whereabouts."

"Against Dixie's dying wishes? Not a chance," I said.

We followed behind him to finish the conversation as he sat the last tubs into the back of the truck. He turned and said, "Dr. Ma'am, you are a lovely lady." He glanced at Tinsley as if to suggest she was something else entirely. "You wouldn't be here if you weren't salt of the earth, and I would understand if you decided not to take him. I feel bad that my sister pushed HER responsibility onto YOU, but it's not mine."

Tinsley and I looked at each other. Outdone by the uncle's ambivalence towards Luke, she turned and said, "Okay, Nay...

So, not only do you have this stranger's only son in your care. He has a 666 birthmark under that matted, little mullet, too?"

Lawson and I looked at Tinsley with a hint of confusion. "Yeah, I said it! He's talking about this kid as if we're dealing with the devil," Tinsley said hysterically. I'm beginning to think Tinsley missed her meds this morning, but she wasn't wrong.

Lawson said from the driver's seat of his truck, "Let me give you my phone number." I handed him my phone, and he punched the number in. "I'm not sure how much help I can be, but you never know."

"Yeah, that part...," said Tinsley with impatience and sarcasm.

With an exasperated sigh, Lawson dropped his head and started the truck. "Charlotte is arranging the funeral services. The least I can do is let you know when everything's been scheduled. How is Luke taking the news?" Lawson asked.

"He doesn't know yet. I was hoping you or someone in the family would tell him," I said with disappointment and irritation. There was an awkward silence, but Lawson was adamant that he would not be the one to deliver the news or take him in.

"I'm truly sorry, Dr. Martinez," he said as he fastened his seatbelt. "You will find an envelope in my sister's room addressed to you, though," he said. With that, Lawson pulled off and drove away.

"What in the world was that?" Tinsley said. "Call Child Services. I told you I had a bad feeling about this, Naomi. Did you hear how he talked about this kid?"

"Tinsley, chill out!" I said." "My goodness, yes, I heard him. Come on, let's go in the house." As we went inside Dixie's house, I received a text reply from Justine.

"OMG..." Justine responded with multiple sad face emojis. She stated Luke was awake and they were having breakfast. She said she would drop off Luke afterward.

I went into Dixie's room, and Tinsley went toward the bathroom. The house was empty now. The only thing left was a Rubbermaid tub. Sitting on top were some hospice papers, an ashtray, and an envelope with my name scrawled on the front.

"Naomi!" Tinsley said, walking toward me. She had a pair of empty pill bottles in her hand. Both bottles have Luke's name printed on them. "I found these in the medicine cabinet," she said. I shook my head at her, given that she'd be snooping around, but I'm glad she did. I took the bottles from her and read them.

"Risperdal."

"Lithium."

Tinsley looked at me curiously, then shouted, "The kid's on fucking lithium – he's a goddamn toddler! We need to call Child Services. Why would this kid be taking psychotropics, Naomi?" Tinsley asked.

I understand the different reasons a kid could be prescribed these types of medications at such an early age. One drug treats aggression and irritability, while the other addresses bipolarity and juvenile mania. I lied rather than explain this to Tins and have her lose her remaining shit completely.

"I'm not sure, but I will get to the bottom of it," I said as I stuffed the pill bottles in my fanny pack. "Let's get out of here and get home. I still have to break this awful news to Luke."

CHAPTER 17

*W*hen Tinsley and I returned to my house, Gio's car was in front of our third garage. When they saw us turn into the driveway, Ferrin and Gio both emerged from the black sportscar. They must have spoken to Tinsley, because I didn't know they were coming over. We all hugged and headed into the house.

"Girl!" Ferrin said. "This is so bizarre. We were just together, and she was alive. Now, she's gone. I'm so sorry, dear," she said, shaking her head from side to side and hugging me.

"Did you have a chance to tell her that you would not take him?" Gio asked.

"No, I didn't. I thought I had more time because I just saw her. She seemed stronger and more alert than she had ever been."

"Is that Luke in a red SUV?" Tinsley asked as she was looking out of the window.

"Yes, that's Justine, the woman who has known them for a while," I replied. "Maybe she will take him," Tinsley said. Luke jumped out of the car as Ferrin, Gio, and Tinsley were bunched together, looking out the window.

"Naomi, is Luke the one with dark hair?" Ferrin asked.

"Yes," I replied.

"Aw, he is so cute!" she said.

"I know," Gio said. "I love him so much."

"Lord, I think I'm going to cry. I feel so sorry for y'all," Ferrin said. I walked outside toward Justine and judging by her eyes, she had been crying.

"Hi, Luke," I said.

"Hi!" he said, smiling at me. Luke is a cute boy with big eyes and cheeks and a head full of coal-black hair that comes to his shoulders. Everything fit perfectly with his round face. "Can I go to the park?" Luke asked.

"Maybe, but I have something I would like to talk to you first. Go on inside and meet my friends," I said.

"Okay," he said as he ran toward the house. "Bye, Luke!" Connor yelled.

"How are you holding up, Naomi?" Justine asked.

"I'm good," I said. "A little overwhelmed by all of this, but I'm okay. I hate that I did not have a chance to tell Dixie that I was not taking Luke."

Justine blew her nose in a napkin and said, "I understand. Luke can be challenging; he's always been that way," Justine said.

"I met Lawson, who clarified he had no interest in taking Luke. He assured me no one in the family would take him either," I said.

"I'm not surprised," Justine said. "I'm not sure she would even want them to have him. She never had a good relationship with any of them, you know. And his father is not in the picture."

"Why does everyone keep saying words like "challenging" when talking about this kid?" I asked out of curiosity.

"Because," Justine said, "it's the truth." She looked at me like she was trying to say more but wouldn't.

"You have known them for quite some time. Would you be

interested in taking him?" I asked, chuckling as if I was pretend-ing...but I was dead serious. She looked shocked and immedi-ately started acting like I insulted her by asking.

"Absolutely not!" she said. "The last time Luke was at my house, he set my attic on fire!"

"Wait, what?" I asked in a concerned tone.

"Yes, he sure did," Justine said. "I understand she wanted someone to take Luke, but she knew that that would have been asking a lot. I understand you have to do what you must, and I'll support whatever decision you make."

She didn't sound that different from Lawson just a bit ago. "I'm not sure what I'm going to do," I said, "but right now, I need to break the news to him. I paused and shook my head. "He'll never get to talk to, kiss, or hug his mother again. I know that's going to be tough on him."

I took a deep breath and thanked Justine for keeping him. She assured me that if I needed information or babysitting help with Luke, she would do what she could.

* * *

I'm no stranger to delivering harsh truths and bad news. It comes with the territory of a medical professional, but this is an eight-year-old boy without a mother. When I walked into the house, Ferrin and Gio were sitting down. Gio had his head in his hand, and Ferrin had a half-smirk on her face. Luke stood in front of Tinsley, as she was looking through his hair.

"What are you doing, Tinsley?" I asked.

"I'm just looking... for a specific... birthmark," she said. Ferrin threw her hands in the air, got up, and went to the kitchen."Girl, stop it," I said. I gently grabbed Luke's hand and walked him to the family room. We sat down.

"Luke, remember I told you I had something to tell you?"

"Yes," he said, looking at me with those big eyes.

"There's no easy way for me to tell you this. Your mom died last night." I was careful not to confuse him with euphemisms or provide details I didn't have.

Luke's reaction was still and quiet. He had no expression on his face to speak of. I rubbed his back gently and asked, "Do you understand what that means, Luke?" He nodded affirmatively.

"There was nothing anyone said or did to make this happen. None of it is your fault, you understand?" Again, he nodded. I looked at him, anticipating something more, but he just looked at the floor.

"Do you have any questions for me?" I asked. "No..." he said. I gestured for him to come over, and I hugged him. "I'm sorry this happened, but you are safe," I said while holding him in my arms.

Gio was at the edge of the family room, ear hustling with a look of concern. He approached us, knelt, and wrapped his arms around us. "If you need anything, Luke, I'm your new tio, Gio, and I'm here for you. Tio means Uncle." Luke smiled and nodded.

Seconds later, Ferrin and Tinsley, who had been spying on us with Gio outside the room, joined in on our tearful group hug. "We're all here for you, Luke," Ferrin said.

"Sweetie, are you okay?" I asked.

"Yeah, I'm okay," he said.

I explained, "You going to live here with me until we figure some things out."

He nodded again and we all moved from the family room towards the bar in my kitchen.

"Naomi..." Luke said. We all paused and looked down at him.

"I do have a question." I think we each expected him to ask something existential or spiritual.

"So, is my mom's truck mine now?"

"Whoa, shiii...," Tinsley muttered the curse beneath her

breath as we all stood there frozen. I couldn't be upset with her. She just verbalized the shocked reaction each of us was having to his completely unexpected inquiry. My best friends looked around at each other and then at me. Luke looked directly into my eyes, awaiting an answer.

"Well, I'm not sure who will have your mom's truck, Luke. You do know you are too young to drive, right?"

"Yeah. Can I *please* go outside now?" he asked with impatience.

At that point, I was entirely taken aback by his indifference. "Well...um... yes, but are you sure you don't want to talk about it?" I asked, my words stammering uncharacteristically.

"No, I just want to go play," he said firmly.

"Alright then. Check-in with me in a couple of hours, okay?" He nodded his head and ran out the front door.

* * *

MY FRIENDS WERE THERE and saw the entire scene play out before their eyes. All I could do then was shake my head, but I'd seen this cold disregard from him before.

"Strange, right?" I asked them rhetorically.

"I TOLD YOU!" Tinsley said.

"Why is this kid not crying?" Ferrin asked.

I responded, "I know, but it's not uncommon for some children to misunderstand or constrain their emotions after suffering trauma like this. It will hit him eventually, and he'll begin to grieve. He needs time."

My friends looked at each other with doubt.

"I still feel like he should have cried,'" Ferrin said.

"Umm, that baby's face was blank like nothing," Gio declared, "...and did I hear him ask if he had just inherited her car? Girl, that's sus!"

Tinsley laughed so hard she had to bend forward to keep

herself upright. We all looked at her, assuming she had something heavy to say.

"Whew, I just can't. That little boy is too much. I know you are the professional here, Naomi, but you've seen the warning signs. If that doesn't tell you something is wrong, I don't know what will!"

She said, "You just told this boy his mother was dead. Any other kid in America would have bawled their eyes out, right? Not this one! His first question is about that broken-down truck in their driveway?!" Just call Child Services and be done with this!"

Ferrin looked on with grave concern, then jumped in. "Hold on, warning signs? What does Tinsley know that we don't? What *issues*, Naomi?"

"Look," I said. "I'm not sure what he has going on, but I need to figure out what I will do with him. I'm going to make the best decision I can because he is a child, and apparently, I'm the only person he has in the entire world now that his mother is gone. I would feel bad if something went wrong as a result of a decision *I* made. He might end up with Child Services, but not before I explore my options."

Gio and Ferrin nodded in agreement while Tinsley stared at me with concern and disapproval. I knew what she was thinking—Naomi was making a huge mistake.

CHAPTER 18

*W*ith everything going on, the last thing I wanted to do was attend the conference, but I wasn't going to cancel at the last minute. I have a strong sense of duty and responsibility, which should be obvious considering how I've handled the Luke situation thus far. Justine was kind enough to come over and watch Luke while I was on campus to deliver my speech. Mentally, it was tough to stay in the moment, but once it was time for me to present, muscle memory kicked in, and I switched into "boss mode."

The standing ovation I received after my presentation proved that I nailed it. Dean Jamison was grateful and made a point to thank me directly. The conference went off without a hitch and was a huge success. I wasn't able to stay for post-conference networking, however. I needed to return home and pick up where I left off with Luke.

I had only been gone a few hours. When I arrived home, Luke was taking a nap. I wanted to believe he was emotionally exhausted from coping with the loss of his mother, but honestly, I didn't know. I had delivered the worst news an adult could ever bear to a child, but he seemed to handle it better than I was.

I replayed his reactions over and over again as I watched him sleep. Given what I'd discovered about his psychiatric history, I didn't trust the 'people handling grief in different ways' explanation.

I decided to connect with the doctor who prescribed Luke's psychotropics, which Tinsley found in Dixie's medicine cabinet the day after she died. I wanted to believe that Dixie would have shared Luke's mental diagnosis with me. She would have mentioned him being seen and evaluated by a mental health professional. "She would've said something... She would have told me. We just didn't have enough time. If she had more time, right?" I had difficulty convincing myself that this was the case. It was yet another red flag, and considering the distance the other family members kept from Luke, I shuddered to think what else I didn't know. "Don't delve deeper into that awful rabbit hole. Make the call and go from there. Maybe they can help him process his feelings better than you," I thought.

It was then that I remembered the envelope Dixie left for me. I hoped there were no more surprises because I wasn't sure I could handle any more. Inside the envelope was a handwritten letter:

To whom this may concern:

My name is Loretta Wade, and I'm writing this letter with a sound mind. I leave my son Luke Wade to Naomi Martinez. Any money and assets upon my death will pass to Naomi Martinez on behalf of my next of kin (Luke Miller). It is my dying wish that under no circumstances do I want ANYONE else (family, friends, or biological father) to have custody of my only child. There has never been a relationship between myself, my son, and my family. I'm pleading with the courts to never award Luke to his father because of his strained relationship with his son and due to abuse, incarceration, and illegal drug use.

My dying wish will allow me peace as I leave this earth and embark on my next journey. I beg the courts to accept this letter as my last will and testament. I suppose there will be a process to challenge this letter for my son's adoption to Naomi Martinez. In that case, I beg the courts to conduct a thorough investigation of the challenging participants, whereas you will undoubtedly find them unworthy of adopting my son.

Sincerely,

Loretta Wade

I paused as the words from her letter set in. "What do you say to something like that!? And, what court will take this as a legally binding statement of her wishes?"

As much as the family had no interest in assuming custody of Luke, Dixie was gravely serious about Luke having nothing to do with them. Her letter pulled me further into a crisis I had no idea was coming a week ago. I folded it and placed it back into the unsealed envelope she'd left behind for me. I wanted to respect her dying wishes, but she certainly hadn't thought about what this responsibility would mean for me or mine.

Just then, my phone lit up with text messages from a number I didn't recognize. The messages read:

Hello Nayome

this is Charlotte Loretta's sister

here are the details for Loretta's funeral

I hope Luke is doing OK I know how close he was to his mom

If I can help in any way, let me know

Her butchering of my name aside, I was stunned by the level of fakery in her texts. "How dare she! *If she can help in any way?!?* She stole her cousin's identity, life savings, and Luke's nest egg... *I hope Luke is doing alright...* despite tossing her nephew's belongings in the trash, and let's not forget— abandoning him for a week." Her audacity enraged me, but it added insult to injury, considering how rapidly Dixie's funeral arrangements were made.

"It's like they couldn't wait for her to die," I thought.

I wasn't feeling Charlotte from the get-go, but I had to ask myself, "What kind of people are these to be so cold and heartless?" At that point, my disdain for the evil sister-cousin extended to everyone in Dixie's family except Luke.

"And how the hell did she get my number anyway!?"

I thought back and deduced that it had to be Lawson. "He must have given my number to her after we crossed paths at the house." Although the message would show that I read it, I decided I wouldn't be dignifying it or Charlotte with a response immediately. I returned to the task at hand: contacting Luke's child psychiatrist.

* * *

I DIALED the number on the side of the pill bottles. The phone rang two times before I heard a female voice say, "Bedlam Mental Health. This is Nancy speaking." I paused and thought, "Seriously? Bedlam? They named their facility *Bedlam*?"

The name alone conjured black-and-white images in my mind: ones of people in straight jackets, padded rooms, and metal caps—images from when the pursuit of scientific understanding was more important than Hippocratic oaths. When I saw the facility's isolation on a map (about 130 miles southwest of Middleton in the middle of nowhere), I was sure I'd pictured the right place. I would have been less surprised if it were called Arkham and Harley Quinn had answered the phone.

I replied, "Hello, Nancy. This is Dr. Naomi Martinez calling. I'm trying to reach Elise McKay. I must speak with her about a patient in my care." I replied.

"Dr. McKay is not available. Would you like her voicemail?" she asked.

"Yes, please. Thank you." I answered.

I left Dr. McKay a voicemail to call me back. Getting information about Luke's condition might be a long shot because of "patient-doctor privilege." Other than the letter, I didn't have a legal basis that allowed me to know his mental health history. I hoped my reputation and credibility as a psychiatrist would help Dr. McKay get past that inconvenient truth.

"One task down," I thought.

The funeral would be held that weekend, so I had a few days to prepare Luke for the worst day of his young life. I decided to watch over him and monitor his emotional state for the rest of the week. After all, this was a lot for a kid to digest, but he'd yet to shed a tear in my presence. And, part of me was still hoping that I might meet some other, non-dysfunctional family member at the funeral. Someone willing to take him in, keep him safe and raise him to be better than his origins. Regardless, I had to stay the course.

Luke and I headed to Gio's boutique to pick up his suit for the funeral. I had already purchased more clothes, toiletries, etc., to get him through the week because he didn't have *anything*. I knew what he looked like before and could guarantee that he would look like a different kid with me.

On our way, I decided that I'd get his hair trimmed. That was interesting because, being a Black woman, I hadn't patronized a salon specializing in white hair. I didn't know where to take him, so I had to get a referral from Tinsley!

Upon her recommendation, I walked into this salon. Although they were friendly, you could see the curious glances. There was a slight time-stop moment as stylists and clients tried to place me within their 'situational context.' I walked through there majestically, holding Luke's hand.

"Welcome! How can we help you?" asked the salon's scheduler.

"Yes, I would like to have his hair trimmed," I said, but before the scheduler could say another word, a full-figured, older woman with bright, red curly hair approached us. By the effort she had put into her makeup, I knew she'd make a point of Luke looking his best. She seemed pleasant enough but didn't formally greet me. Her first words were directed to Luke. "I can trim your hair, hon," she said. I let her microaggression go, and we followed to her hair-dressing station.

As she trimmed Luke's hair, I sat down and began reading emails on my phone. However, I sensed something. It was the stylist looking at me through her mirror. "She's buffering," I chuckled. I knew exactly what she was trying to figure out — she wanted to know the connection between us. In Big Red's mind, it simply didn't compute that a Black woman would walk in with a white kid for a haircut. But she was trying to figure it out or muster the courage to ask.

By this point, I was entertained by her angst. I had no intention of making this easy for her by volunteering an explanation. If knowing was that important to her, she'd have to ask, and I was curious to see how long it would take her to do it.

She looked back down at Luke when she noticed me, noticing her. She began making small talk with him, and I shifted in my seat a bit to hear them better. The red-haired stylist asked about his age and where he went to school. A few minutes passed, and then came the million-dollar question - the real question she wanted to ask.

"Is that your nanny right there - pointing into the mirror at me?"

I looked back at her reflection with a priceless scowl and an over-dramatized eye roll. "Nanny? Really?" I thought to myself. What about this situation makes her believe I'm the nanny? In her small mind, seeing a Black woman bringing a white kid to an all-white salon could only make sense to her if I were his nanny. But, if this were the other way around and our races reversed, would she have reached the same conclusion?

Not a chance.

But, there's also little chance I'd bring a Black kid here to get their hair done.

I answered before Luke could get a word out.

"No. I'm not his nanny, his maid, or the help. What if I told you he was my son? Would you still have that look on your face?" I was looking into her eyes but speaking to everyone in the salon indirectly. I dramatized the offense of her question because I was having a bit of fun making her face match her hair.

"Now I'm curious. What's easier for you to believe?" I figured if she was bold enough to make a racist assumption like that, then she should damn well be prepared to answer the question.

"I...I didn't mean to offend you," she stuttered. "I don't know why I said that, but I assure you, I did not mean anything by it."

I decided to take the high road yet again. I wasn't in the mood for a teaching moment. Educating this woman on the racist, bigoted, and privileged nature of her offensive assumption wouldn't be a valuable use of my precious energy. Not on a good day, and certainly not with all I had on my plate trying to get Luke ready for his mother's funeral.

"I'm sure you didn't. Just finish with his hair, please, and we'll be on our way."

Despite being as ignorant as a bat with a blindfold, she did a fantastic job with Luke's hair. As I surveyed his new hairdo, I was glad I didn't ask for his hair to be cut shorter. The thought had crossed my mind, but "Not my place to make that decision," I said. After the salon, I decided that home would be our next stop. I called to let Gio know.

"It's fine. I have the perfect ensemble for him. I'll come by tomorrow."

I needed to take a load off. We grabbed take-out from his favorite drive-thru restaurant, and he was content to play video games in the twins' room. I found myself lying in bed, looking at the ceiling and asking, "Why me?" You hear strange things happening to people all the time, but this was unimaginable. I explained to Kinney last night that I felt sorry for Dixie and the entire situation, but I began to feel angry at that moment.

I was angry at Dixie for putting me in this situation. She put my name down as an emergency contact without knowing me. By doing that, she had taken away my ability to choose if I was okay with her doing so. Then, she left me responsible for deciding her son's future with family members who didn't want anything to do with him. She did not consider how this would affect my family and me.

At the time, I had no idea what tomorrow would hold. Dixie's memorial would be open to all visitors. I hoped the ceremony would bring other members of Dixie's extended family that would feel motivated or duty-bound to care for Luke. But, the weight of her dying wish still sat upon my shoulders, alone.

CHAPTER 19

I awoke not knowing what to expect — from the funeral, the family members that might be in attendance, and most importantly, from Luke himself. Kinney was adamant about coming home, but I insisted he stay with the kids in Belize. I wouldn't allow this situation to disrupt my family's summer vacation more than it already had. I told myself, "I just need to get through today so I can get back to my own life."

"Luke, did you see the shampoo and conditioner I left for you?" I asked before he got in the shower.

"Yes," he said as he turned on the shower.

Indeed, there were big things about Luke's behavior and demeanor that I couldn't make sense of, but there were also little things. For instance, he had to be reminded to do basic things repeatedly. I have my own boys, and they didn't require the level of micromanagement that Luke did concerning hygiene. He hated to bathe. My children know to make their beds, wash their faces, and brush their teeth before eating breakfast when they wake up. Luke would wake up, eat, and go outside wearing whatever he went to bed in if I'd let him. He wants to eat junk food all day and sneak downstairs to snack voraciously at night. He would leave his things wherever and refuse to pick up after himself without a slight attitude. "Whoever takes him today better have a lot of structure in place, or he's going to run all over them," I thought.

That was wishful thinking, to say the least.

After a bit, Luke and I were dressed for the funeral. Luke was a good-looking kid, and he cleaned up nicely. He seemed to like what he saw in the mirror. I hoped it would encourage him to do it more often but on his own. "Tio Gio is going to be proud of this suit, Luke! You look like a million bucks." He grinned at me while admiring himself a bit more. I knelt down and asked, "How are you feeling?"

"Good," he said, tying the black dress shoes that Gio had brought over for him.

"I know we've talked about today a couple of times, but if you need anything or have any questions while we're at the funeral, I will do my best."

"Okay," he said. I hugged him and told him I'd be ready to go in just a few minutes.

It had been days since I told Luke about his mother's death. While Luke rarely answered me with more than one or two words, I was highly concerned about how he'd behave in the coming moments at the funeral home. Luke's emotional state was enigmatic. Thus far, he seemed completely unfazed. So much so that I figured her loss hadn't hit him yet. Seeing her today, lying in her casket, could be his breaking point, but I felt prepared to support him.

I looked in the mirror as I finished getting ready. For a split second, I wished I had someone to support me the way I was supporting him. The chief justice spoke, "Don't wallow, Naomi. You'll have your time to mourn... eventually."

She... I mean, I was right. It was time for us to go.

* * *

WE ARRIVED at the funeral home, and to my surprise, the lot was full of cars. Tinsley, Gio, and Ferrin were going to meet me there. I knew I would need their support, if only for the comfort of their friendly, familiar faces in a room full of strangers. We exited my car, and I reminded Luke that I was there for him.

He shook his head up and down, gesturing that he understood, and we hugged before making our way in. As we approached the doors, I took a deep breath, bracing myself for whatever the other side of this door may bring. I hoped that by the end of the ceremony, I would have the names and numbers of additional family members capable and interested in assuming custody.

Luke and I held hands and walked through the doors. It was impossible not to notice this large, somber space filled with white faces...no people of color except me. The voices we heard upon entering the room quieted to whispers as we made our way down the aisles. Stares followed. Luke's grip around my hand tightened. People who recognized him were taken aback by how great he looked.

We continued down the seemingly endless rows of seats past more and more faces that neither he nor I recognized. Dixie was resting peacefully in a shiny, black casket. To the left side of us were several rows of chairs filled with people. For someone who didn't feel loved, there were over 100 people there to pay their respects. I hoped she was looking down on the procession to see all the people who came to celebrate her life and send her home.

Luke and I walked up to the casket, and there she was. Dixie looked beautiful in her white floral dress. Her hair was curled on the ends, just like it was in my dream. The funeral home was silent as Luke surveyed his mother lying there. Although our backs faced everyone, I could feel their eyes on us, waiting and watching curiously to see what Luke might do.

I was the most curious of all. I braced myself for his emotional meltdown. But Luke just stood there, staring at her.

"She looks beautiful, doesn't she?" I asked.

"Yeah. She looks nice," Luke said.

"Are you okay, Luke?" I asked, concerned with how overwhelming this could be for him.

"I'm okay," he said. He continued looking at her as if studying her face and memorizing the details.

"Is there anything you want to say to her? It's okay if you do. I can give you some time with her by yourself if you'd like."

"That's okay... I'm okay," he said.

I nodded, and we turned around to sit down. Just like I thought, everyone in the room was watching us. Perhaps they were expecting a more dramatic display for him. True to form, he didn't cry at all. He was impressively stoic. But, for a child this young, I was more alarmed by his reaction than relieved.

"Luke!" A child's voice called for him. We turned around, and there were several people he recognized. "Hey, those are my friends from school," he whispered. He started smiling and waving back at them as other mourners smiled at the cute moment.

"Aw, that was nice of them to show up. Let's go back there so you can talk to your friends and thank them for coming."

As we approached the back of the room, I caught several people looking at me. Some had curious, cynical looks, while others signaled warmth with polite nods or sympathetic smiles. I found a seat in the back of the room where I would have a full view of the ceremony and keep an eye on Luke as he visited with his classmates.

"Go ahead. I'll be right here."

Luke was in remarkably good spirits despite his mother lying mere feet away from him in her casket. He was smiling and laughing with other kids brought to pay their respects and support the little guy in his moment of loss.

Meanwhile, people, including Ferrin, Tinsley, and Gio, were still piling into the funeral. They didn't have a difficult time spotting me — because I was waving my arms to get their attention and guide them over. I was delighted they arrived. I was now one of three people of color in the room, and we had at least one ally in Tinsley. That would be more than enough for me, at least for now.

I greeted them each with a warm embrace. They sat beside me, and we watched as people entered and found their seats.

"Well, it looks like she knew lots of people!" Gio whispered.

"I was thinking the same thing. Her whole town turned out to say goodbye," Ferrin responded.

Tinsley was texting on her phone, looking preoccupied as usual.

"See the lady standing in the corner with the green blazer? That's Charlotte, Dixie's sister," I said.

"Where? Which one?" Tinsley asked abruptly while multitasking.

"In the corner there. That's the sister who stole Dixie's lottery money," I said, reminding her of what I told them.

"Ooohhh," they all said at the same time.

"Why is she staring in Luke's direction like that?" Ferrin asked.

"I'm not sure. She hasn't spoken to him since we arrived. Not even a hello."

"Really?" Ferrin said.

"I'm not surprised," Tinsley said. Gio just sat there, shaking his head with a frown.

"This family is so strange," Tinsley quipped. Before she returned to her text conversation, another mourner caught her attention.

"Naomi, isn't that the guy we spoke with at her house that

day?" She discreetly pointed to a man approaching the casket in a black suit.

"It sure is. That's Lawson," I said.

"Who is Lawson?" Gio asked.

"Dixie's adopted brother." Gio squinted as if focusing on getting a better look, then disinterestedly rolled his eyes. "That suit does nothing for his physique." We giggled under our breath.

"Luke seems to be handling all this well," Tinsley said with a hint of suspicion.

"Yes, he is doing much better than I anticipated, but someone will need to find him a good therapist."

"Well," Ferrin said, "I guess that will be your job, Naomi." Tinsley and Gio chuckled quietly at her witty remark. I just shook my head before scanning the room as I had been since moving from the front of the venue to the back rows.

I noticed a man walking quickly across the front of Dixie's remembrance. Unlike the others, he didn't pause to acknowledge her or the casket, nor did he speak to anyone up there paying their respects. I realized he was walking toward the back of the funeral home and headed directly to where my three friends and I were sitting.

"Naomi, who the hell is this?" Ferrin asked defensively. The man standing before our pew was slim and unshaven, five-foot-eight with a jet-black mop-top like the Beatles. He had a black eye with a red spot on his sclera, matching his flannel shirt. By my standards, he wasn't dressed appropriately for the occasion. Regardless, he was too close for comfort, and his body language was hostile. Bless her heart, Ferrin stood up like a bodyguard and was ready for action.

"I don't know which of you has my boy, but my son is coming with me!" The man spoke sternly, trying to intimidate us, but his features were strikingly familiar.

I knew exactly who this was...

CHAPTER 20

"This must be that deadbeat, Cash that I've heard so much about...Luke's father. He looked more like 'change,' but whatever," I thought.

I stood up from my seat and addressed the angry little man. "I think you're looking for me," I said with my chest, looking directly into his functioning eye. I entered the funeral prepared for anything, so I wasn't intimidated. "My name is Naomi Martinez. And you are...?"

"Cash," he said, with his little chest puffed out. He was obviously proud of his name.

"Well, Cash... I cannot let you take Luke anywhere. If you want your son, I suggest you obtain an attorney and do this correctly." He stood there pondering his next move, and I could only hope he didn't try to *fight* me. Dixie made it clear that 1) he enjoyed hitting women, 2) he was a drug addict, and 3) he'd come out of the woodwork after she died if he thought he could gain from taking Luke. With that combination, there was no telling what this idiot might do. He looked at my squad and me a little longer, smirked and backed away with his hands up.

It took a moment for us to settle down and regain our

composure. "Who the hell does he think he is?" Ferrin said. "I was ready to match his good eye up with that blacked one, walking back here trying to be tough."

Tinsley, who evidently had something in her purse just in case, said, "I need a drink." She leaned down to take a sip from a tiny flask in her Birkin bag! After recovering from her stiff shot, she said, "I told you, Naomi, you have got to wash your hands of this mess."

"Not now, Tinsley," I said.

Gio was sitting there looking a little nervous. "We dressed too good to deal with trash like him today," Gio said.

Luke noticed the brief but uncomfortable exchange. I don't know if he knew what was happening, but to my surprise, he looked at me with genuine concern. I gestured to let him know that I was okay.

Just then, there was a scream that got all of our attention.

"You killed my sister, you son of a bitch!" It was Charlotte, yelling at Cash.

"Get out of my fucking face!" Cash yelled.

"Get the hell out of here! You're not welcome here!" Charlotte screamed.

"You shut your fucking mouth!" Cash said as they exchanged sprinkles of saliva on each other's faces. All I could say to myself was, "Eww!"

Some guy was holding one of Charlotte's arms, trying to pull her back, but Charlotte broke loose and struck Cash in the face with her fist.

"Oh, my God," Ferrin said. "She just hit him in the face!" Cash grabbed Charlotte's arms to keep her from hitting him again. Before you know it, they began tussling violently. Charlotte had the height, weight, and anger advantage, but Cash somehow managed to push Charlotte away. She reached backward to regain her balance and stumbled backward into the casket!

The whole room gasped as Dixie and the casket literally rocked side to side!

"Oh my god!" I prayed that it didn't tip over. When I say everyone was mortified, that would be the understatement of the century. No one could believe what they were seeing. I had never witnessed anything like that in all my life. "This kind of thing only happens in movies, not real life!" I thought.

The people that should have been top of mind to take Luke were literally fist-fighting at his mother's funeral—no self-control and certainly no respect for Luke, Dixie, or anyone else there to say goodbye. Several men in dark suits ran toward the fight scene as people scurried and pushed toward the exits.

The funeral had descended into complete chaos.

I looked across the venue and spotted Luke near the front of the remembrance. I saw him crying and wailing at the top of his lungs while his kinfolk continued to scuffle violently. I tried pushing past the flow of people to get to him when I saw Justine, who was much closer to the crying boy.

"Justine!" I yelled. "Take Luke out the back and meet me outside!" I wasn't sure if she heard me completely, but she nodded, picked him up, and headed for the exits nearest the front. I told Gio I would meet them at the house, and I continued pushing my way forward.

Charlotte and Cash were still screaming and fighting, and another man had joined the uproar. I thought it was Kyle, but it may have been Lawson. At that point, I had one focus — getting to Luke and getting out of there. But I couldn't help but watch this train wreck as I moved closer to the action. Charlotte was on Cash's back with her legs wrapped around his waist, landing punch after punch on Cash's matted mop top. As she walloped him, I wondered, "What happened to her shoes?"

Blood was running down Cash's face from a gash Charlotte opened on his head. He was on the losing end of this battle, but judging by his black eye, he was no stranger to losing fights.

Not far from them was a crying woman lying on the floor. Apparently, she had been in the middle of the fight. Her dress was hiked above her thighs and she was missing her footwear like Charlotte. Her multicolored hair was sloppily strewn all over her head and face. It had to be Jennifer.

"What was Jennifer doing down there?!? Cash must have landed a punch or two after all. These people are completely nuts!" I thought.

I imagined Dixie looking down on all this. "How would she feel? What a travesty. But, given what she told me, she might have expected it." To think that a few minutes earlier, Charlotte and Cash almost knocked her out of her casket. I couldn't fathom what that would have done to us. Luke would have been scarred for the rest of his life had she tumbled onto the floor. Lord, I was scarred just thinking about it.

I was surprised to look behind me and find my loyal squad following me through the crowd. I didn't bother to ask, but they weren't going to leave me in here alone. We continued forward and eventually gathered near the rear exits of the venue. Yes, we should have left, but watching this shit show from backstage was priceless.

"Girl, these white people are crazy!" Gio whispered. Tinsley overheard him and couldn't let the remark go unnoticed. "This isn't a *white* people thing, G. We don't have a monopoly on crazy. These are just classless, country lowlifes that happen to be white."

Gio rolled his eyes and whispered, "Hmm, like I said..." Ferrin wanted to holler but held her laughter in, and I just put up my hands as we watched the men in suits attempt to pry Charlotte off of Cash's back.

At that point, we could hear sirens approaching the funeral home. "It's about time the police got here," Tinsley said as we exited the building. I saw Justine with Luke and Connor in her car on the other side of the parking lot. "We'll just meet you at my house," I shouted. She gave me a thumbs-up and started driving. Luke just looked at me from her backseat.

I hoped everyone involved in ruining Dixie's funeral would be arrested, but we wouldn't be there to find out.

* * *

I DROVE down the street feeling sorry that Luke and I couldn't stay for the entire funeral. Not only was it unbelievable, but it was completely selfish and disrespectful. None of them considered how their behavior would make Luke feel. None of them put his emotional well-being ahead of their own pity and self-interest. I should have predicted it. I saw all the warning signs and red flags. It was a recipe for disaster that boiled over at the worst place and worst time possible — in front of Luke and his classmates. They'll talk about that funeral for the rest of their lives.

Then, I declared, "None of these cretins are fit to care for this kid. No more voices, no more debate, no more doubt. He will stay with us, and whoever wants him will need to fight me in court. Luke did not deserve this. He deserved stability in his life. He had been in and around chaos and confusion for too long, and enough was enough."

I wasn't sure what Kinney might say, but Luke's only option besides us would be Child Services. There was no way any of his family was going to get custody. And Lawson, the only sane relative I'd met thus far, was adamant that he wouldn't take him in (despite his own experience as an adopted child). I shook my head at all of it as I pulled into the driveway of my house, which wasn't far from the funeral home.

Justine's red SUV was already parked, so I hurried over from my car, opened the back door of the red SUV, and found Luke sitting there with his head hung low. I reached in, and he reached back with his eyes full of tears.

Luke and I hugged and held him for several minutes as he continued sobbing. As he cried into my shoulder, I felt myself getting angrier and angrier. I couldn't remember the last time I'd been this upset. Luke's eyes and face were red, and his voice was hoarse from screaming in horror at what had just happened.

"Naomi... I'm so sorry. I can't believe... I've never seen anything like that. Leave it up to Charlotte and Derry to cause a scene." I could tell Justine had been crying because her eyes were swollen. As I thought about it, Justine had spent a lot of time crying, and I had to remind myself that she too was grieving. She considered Dixie a friend, and in actuality, she had been more helpful to Luke and me than anyone in his own family.

"Dixie told me his father would show up if he thought there was money involved," I said.

Justine asked. "What did he say to you... back there before all hell broke loose?"

"He thought he was going to show up and take Luke, I guess."

"Oh, my goodness," Justine said, with her hands over her mouth. "I'm so sorry," and she began to sob. "I have known Dixie and Luke for a long time, and she tried desperately to keep Luke as far away from Derry as possible.

"Derry?" I asked.

"That's Cash. He named himself "Cash" because he thinks it makes him look cool, and the idiot spells it with a "K," but his real name is Derry Miller. He was always abusive to her and never took care of Luke...ever!" she yelled in frustration. Charlotte had the right idea, but I'm so mad that this is Luke's last memory of his mother."

I nodded. At least Justine would be able to leave and put this behind her. This day added a whole new layer of complexity that I'd have to help Luke reconcile and move past.

"Well, Justine, I'm going to take Luke inside. We've had a long day. I appreciate you bringing him here," I said.

"My pleasure," she said as she hugged Luke and kissed him on his cheek.

"Go on inside, Luke." He ambled through the garage and into the house. I felt like Justine needed a hug, but I wanted to be careful of how much empathy I expressed toward her. I mean, the last time I showed compassion to someone I barely knew, it landed me in the front row of a shit show.

Tinsley, Ferrin, and Gio pulled up as Justine was driving off. We all went into the house together. They headed to the kitchen, and I made my way to Luke, who was standing in the observatory looking out the window. I approached him slowly. That afternoon was the first time Luke had shown any visible emotion through the entire situation.

"Luke?"

"Hmmm.

"I'm sorry that you had to see that today. It was disrespectful to you and your mom." He nodded his head but continued to gaze out the window blankly.

"None of that was your fault. Do you understand?"

"Yes," he said.

"Let's get you changed. We need to get something to eat. And then you can play Minefort."

"*Minefort?*" He turned and looked at me with a silly grin. "I think you mean Minecraft or Fortnite, Naomi. Not Minefort!" He thought that was too funny.

I smiled. "Yeah, OK. Fortmight. Nitecraft, whatever it's called!"

He cracked up some more as he ran up the stairs to get changed.

I took my heels off and sat down. It was silent for a few minutes. The events of the past few hours started replying in my mind. My hands began to shake as I thought about what could have been and how much worse things could have gone at the funeral.

Tinsley, Gio and Ferrin came into the observatory with drinks and poured one for me. No one rushed to speak. We all sat there, taking in the view. Gio broke the silence.

"Naomi, I have never seen anything like that before." He whispered, "I thought someone was pranking us or something."

"How is Luke doing?" Ferrin asked.

"He is doing okay under the circumstances," I said.

"I thought I had some mentally unstable family members," Tinsley said sarcastically. "Even they would not have acted like that at a funeral...my God!"

"Did you see that lady hit Luke's daddy in the head with that big clog?" Ferrin said as she chuckled. "I was sure he was going to be knocked out. But I have got to hand it to him — he kept swinging and caught her with a right hook, and down she went!" Now, Ferrin's giggle turned to a full-blown laugh. Gio and Tinsley laughed as well. That would explain why Jennifer was on the floor shoeless. It would also explain the bloody gash pouring out of Cash's mop top.

Luke came down the stairs after getting changed. "Can I go play outside for a while?" he asked.

"Sure, you can, but I want you to check in with me in an hour. Where are you going?"

"To the park," he said.

"Well, be careful," I said as Luke ran out the door.

"He really is cute," Tinsley said. "But I still would send him away. It's just too much work. Let someone else deal with him," she said.

"I've decided. I'm going to let him stay with us for the time being."

Tinsley, Ferrin, and Gio looked at me with grave concern. "Are you sure about that, Nay?" Gio asked.

"No," I said. "But, I feel like this kid has been through a lot, and he has horrible people around him. This is a temporary option until I figure something else out."

"I understand where you're coming from," Ferrin nodded.

"I don't!" Tinsley interjected sharply.

Ferrin rolled her eyes at Tinsley's curt reaction before asking whether I had consulted Kinney about my decision. "I'll call him later. He will be appalled when I tell him about the funeral."

Tinsley poured herself more wine. "I'll just come out and say it... Have you given the 'Black lady raising a white kid' scenario any thought?! Are you up for all the challenges that will come along with that? I know you and Kinney are great people and wonderful parents, but this is completely different."

Ferrin asked, "What are you talking about, Tinsley? We see white women with Black kids all the time, being praised as if they are superheroes because they took a Black kid into their home. There will be some challenges, but Naomi and Kinney can handle them."

Tinsley sipped her wine and held her tongue. Ferrin could sense her desire to say something else and dangled a lure. "Tell me something, Tins. When you see white women with Black kids, do you question whether they are 'capable' or 'up to the challenge'? I'll bet good money that you don't!"

"Settle down, Ferrin. That is not what I meant," Tinsley said, rolling her eyes.

"Then what did you mean, Ms. Tinsley?" Ferrin asked.

She took another sip from her wine glass. "I know you guys are going to 'cancel' me after this," she said as she air-quoted with her fingers.

"Oh no, she didn't!" Gio bristled, shifted in his seat, and grabbed his wine glass with anticipation.

"I just think white kids should be raised with white families, and Black kids should be raised with Black families because it makes everyone's life easier," Tinsley said.

"Unless you are Angelina Jolie," Gio said as he laughed.

"Gio, stop playing. Tinsley, what the hell are you talking about?" Ferrin asked.

Tinsley explained, "Culturally, white people can't teach a Black kid anything about being Black. Black people can't teach white kids anything about being white."

Ferrin was outdone. "Girl, you just gone sit here and ignore hundreds of years of American history? I bet your parents, especially your grandparents, were raised by somebody Black. What, you thought 'The Help' was just a movie?" Ferrin asked. "Look what happened to Naomi when she took Luke to get his haircut... at a salon that *you* recommended. They thought she was his nanny!?! And here you are, sitting in her house, doing the same thing!"

"No, I am not!" Tinsley shouted as she stood up out of her chair. "I'm insulted by what you are implying, Ferrin!" Tinsley's face started to turn red as her eyes filled with tears.

"I'm not suggesting anything, dear," Ferrin said. "It's just that you *sound* like a racist sometimes, and you don't even realize it."

"Okay, ladies, take it down a notch," I said. It was too late for that. Tinsley had tears streaming down her face. If looks could kill, Ferrin would've dropped dead.

"Oh, here we go. Come on with the white woman's tears! They aren't going to save you from this conversation today," Ferrin said, sitting back in her chair and taking a sip from her wine glass.

"Ferrin, you are too ignorant and angry to understand what I'm trying to say!" Tinsley yelled.

"That's enough!" I said.

Tinsley sniffled one more time, and then the tears turned to flames. "I am not a fucking racist, bitch!" Tinsley said as she slammed her hands on the table and leaned toward Ferrin.

Ferrin popped out of her seat, and suddenly, I was in the middle of them with my arms extended, trying to keep them separated as best I could.

Tinsley and Ferrin bump heads often, but never to this degree. "Look, guys. It's been a long day, and I think we are all tired," I said, trying to diffuse the situation.

"She called me a racist. Naomi, you know I'm not a racist. I have dated Black men, and my best friend is Black," Tinsley pointed toward me. Ferrin's expression was priceless, and I hung my head when she said it, too.

"Okay, okay," Gio said. "Let it go, guys. We are all friends here. Let's take a breath. Ferrin didn't actually call you a racist, but Tinsley... You do need to be canceled for calling Ferrin out her name like that." Gio's wasn't wrong, but Tinsley was past the point of correction and clearly felt isolated among the three of us.

"I...I...I can't...I have to go." She grabbed her purse.

"No, Tinsley, don't go," I said.

"Naomi, I need to get home and prepare for work tomorrow."

"Well, let me walk you to the door," I said.

"Bye, guys," Tinsley said as she blew a kiss toward the table where Gio and Ferrin were sitting. Her eyes were swollen, and her mascara was smeared from crying.

"Bye," Gio said. Ferrin didn't say a word or look in her direction. She sipped her wine and looked the opposite way.

As I walked Tinsley into the foyer, I attempted some damage control with my best white friend in the world. "You know she did not mean those things the way you took them, Tinsley."

"Yes, she did. I don't have a racist bone in my body, Naomi," Tinsley muttered.

"Racism doesn't live in your thin bones, Tinsley—it lives in your ignorant spirit," Ferrin shouted from the other room.

"Fuck you, Ferret!"

On that note, I motioned her out the door hastily. I thought, "Ok, that was good, but I'll never admit it. And if Ferrin came around that corner hot, I'd have to let Tinsley take that L all by herself."

"I love Black people, and you know that... I don't see color, and you know that," said Tinsley wearily as we headed to her car.

"Ugh, Tinsley, I thought. She really doesn't get it, but today is not the day." I thanked her for supporting me through this ordeal and told her to get home safely. We'd have to finish this conversation eventually.

I walked back into the house after sending Tinsley off. Ferrin asked Gio, "Remind me... Did Crybaby Barbie call me an ignorant bitch when I showed immunity to her tear attack? Some ignorant mess came out of her mouth, but that was just vile."

Gio and I both laughed. Gio nodded before explaining, "Umm, Barb called you a ferret, if memory serves... you know, cause your name is spelled F.E.R...,"

She glared at us both, daring us to laugh. We smiled but thought better of laughing because Tinsley's words cut Ferrin deep. Gio pursed his lips and continued, "Ferrin, I commend you for taking the high road. Don't stoop to her level." He motioned his glass to hers, and they clinked gently before taking another sip of wine together.

After a pause, Ferrin spoke. "She's just lucky I'm blessed and highly favored. But she won't receive the same grace I showed her next time. I promise you that. Today was about you, Naomi. Just remember that."

I hugged Ferrin long and told her I appreciated her grace, poise, and support. "I've had enough chaos to last the rest of the year. First, the funeral, and now you two. I'm weak!"

They laughed and agreed. Gio said, "I have a project to finish, so I'm heading back to the boutique for a while. Come on, Ferrin. I'll take you home. She rolled her eyes when she remembered that she and Tinsley rode to the funeral together and shook her head. We giggled and said our goodbyes for the night.

Luke was approaching the house as they were leaving. He waved goodbye to my friends as they drove away. We walked into the house and discussed our dinner plans.

"Luke, are you ready to eat? I'm thinking of pizza. What about you?"

"Yep. Can we get cheese and pepperoni?" he asked excitedly.

"We sure can," I replied.

CHAPTER 21

$\mathcal{T}$he day after the funeral, I recall waking up as if I hadn't slept a wink. I was up late on the phone with Kinney, filling him in on all the chaos from the day's events. He felt awful for Luke but was more concerned about me. I told him not to worry and that Luke and I would be going to see his psychiatrist in a couple of days. I explained to Kinney that I wanted Luke to get the help he needed so he could work through the trauma of losing his mom. "The doctor should have his records, and this will help me learn about him and why he was placed on those medications in the first place."

But in the meantime, I knew I needed to sit down with Luke to remind him of the ground rules for staying in my house. You see, he didn't come home until it was dusky and dark last night, even after I made it clear that he needed to be home before nightfall. He was going to learn that I ran a tighter ship. I didn't allow my own children to run around freely all day without checking in. The rules wouldn't be different for him under any circumstances — trauma or otherwise. I already knew how much he needed structure in his life, but coming and going as he pleased (at all hours of the day or night) would never fly with me.

Beyond that, I still needed to learn the basics about this kid. For instance, what grade is he in? What type of allergies does he have? What doesn't he like besides structure? And proper hygiene?

This entire situation was overwhelming. It felt like I was in a bad dream and unable to wake from it. Nonetheless, I hoped Dixie was finally at peace. Don't get me wrong. For a moment, I had kicked myself for being too late to tell Dixie I wouldn't take Luke. Then, a part of me began to believe that maybe the timing was exactly as fate would have it. My presence in her and Luke's life, albeit brief and essentially out of nowhere, granted her some degree of peace. Maybe I helped her let go of her fear and guilt on top of the cancer. And that allowed her to end her earthly journey and joyfully begin her next in the hereafter.

In the same breath, I thought how ironic it was that I would be so immersed in her feelings, given that she hadn't ever considered mine. Ultimately, all I was left with was the responsibility of steering the rest of her only son's young life. "Damn you, Dixie," I thought inside my mind.

A couple of relatively uneventful days had passed, and Luke and I were scheduled to visit Dr. McKay, the psychiatrist who prescribed Luke his medications. Before that visit, I hadn't fully experienced what it felt like to be on the opposite side of 'seeing a shrink.'

Usually, people would be coming to see me, not the other way around. I remember genuinely hoping this doctor would provide a history lesson on Luke because I was starting from scratch and needed as much information as possible about this child.

"Luke, do you remember being here?" I asked.

"A little," he said.

"Do you remember the last time you were here?"

"No, I just remember coming here," he said as he flipped through a magazine.

A younger woman who looked to be in her late thirties with blond hair stood there smiling."Hi, Luke," she said, "Remember me? I'm Dr. McKay. It's been a while since I've seen you." Luke returned the hello with an unemotional wave.

Dr. McKay glanced at Luke, then looked at me warmly before extending her hand and asking, "May I ask who you are?" Before I answered her, I leaned down toward Luke and gently said, "There is a play area across the hall. You go over there until Dr. McKay and I finish talking, alright?" Luke nodded and rapidly made his way to the play area.

"Dr. McKay, I'm Naomi Martinez. I came to see you because I found these prescriptions," and I handed her the empty pill bottles. "I was hoping you could provide some background information on Luke and his conditions."

Dr McKay looked at the bottles and asked, "Where is Luke's mom?

"Sadly, she passed away recently."

"Oh," she said, shaking her head. "I'm so sorry to hear that. She seemed so sad the few times I saw her. I guess you deal with this a lot in your line of work."

Confused by her statement, I responded, "I don't understand. What do you mean in my line of work? Our line of work?" I asked.

Her facial expression showed confusion briefly before she proceeded to clarify, "Well, as a social worker, I figured you deal with this type of situation more often than you probably would like to."

It was easy to see the confidence she had by incorrectly assigning my role in this play to that of a supporting cast member and not the heroine of the tale.

"With all due respect to social workers, Dr. McKay, I'm a

psychiatrist, just like you. I'm sure I mentioned that in my voicemail."

She immediately started shifting in her seat. I could see the realization dawn on her. "Wait, are you *the* Dr. Naomi Martinez," as she reached for a copy of my book from a nearby shelf.

I modestly nodded and said, "Yep, that's me."

Her face turned as red as the small wheel of cheese sitting on her desk. "Oh, I'm *so* sorry, I just..."

I waved her off from finishing the apology and said, "Look, I'm hoping you can provide me with context or background to understand why Luke was prescribed these particular medications."

"Sure, I understand." Dr. McKay said. "I can imagine how hard it must have been for his mom, dealing with Luke. May I ask how she passed?"

"She had a rare form of cancer," I said. She shook her head as she retrieved a file from a nearby drawer.

"Okay, let's take a look here," Dr. McKay said as she opened the relatively thick file folder. Dr. McKay began to read aloud from pages in the file:

"Loretta was a single mother, and the father's whereabouts are unknown. As an infant, Luke showed signs of strain. He cried often and inconsolably. Later, he started displaying signs of behavior disorders as early as two years old. He was placed on Ritalin and assigned an in-home behavior specialist three days a week. However, his mother felt neither the sessions nor the medications were working. When upset, he started banging his head on the cabinets and floors. Then, he'd hold his breath for substantial periods of time. We prescribed Luke stronger medications to stabilize some of his behaviors. Luke has never responded to structure and was defiant most of the time."

She looked up from the file and removed her reading spectacles before mentioning, "His mother stopped bringing him about seven months ago, and it looks like we have not refilled his medication since then. Could it be possible he was seeing another doctor?" she asked.

"It's possible, but I doubt it," I responded before asking my own question. "So, what are his exact diagnoses?"

Dr. McKay began reading off a list I thought might never end. "Attention-Deficit Hyperactivity Disorder (ADHD), Oppositional Defiant Disorder (ODD), Conduct Disorder, Intermittent Explosive Disorder (IED) and Disruptive Mood Dysregulation Disorder (DMDD). Of course, I would recommend having him reevaluated," Dr. McKay said before revealing that she had increased the dosages of his medications seven months back because of his age.

"Dr. Martinez, even then, showed signs of predominantly hyperactive impulsiveness. There were also reports from Ms. Wade and his school teachers that the child exhibited extreme anger, hallucinations, and frequent temper tantrums."

I was taken aback by what I was hearing. There were so many more things going on with this kid than I suspected.

Dr. McKay returned her reading glasses to her eyes and continued from the seemingly endless file. "Here it says he displayed vindictive behaviors, such as bullying, destroying public and private property, and almost compulsive lying."

"Damn! This is an extensive file for an eight-year-old!" I thought.

As Dr. McKay continued reading, I started thinking of everyone who seemed uninterested in keeping Luke. Why would immediate family – sisters and cousins like Charlotte and Jennifer, show no compassion or warmth for this boy? How could they, in good conscience, abandon him for a week without batting an eye? Why would seemingly empathetic relatives like Lawson turn their back on their young kin? Why would lifelong friends of Dixie's like Justine accuse Luke of heinous acts like setting her attic on fire?

Now that I had some trustworthy information from an unbiased source, I could more reasonably understand why people treated Luke like Damian from The Omen. That all too familiar question and feeling came back again. "Naomi, what have you gotten yourself into!?"

This time, however, I wasn't retreating or looking for alternatives to solve my quandary. The information Dr. McKay provided helped me understand the full extent of my journey by taking Luke into my home.

Some of my newfound confidence stemmed from my depth of expertise. Having specialized in a wide array of behavior disorders and their treatments, I understood how many of these illnesses and ailments present as sociopathy or psychopathy in adulthood. Children like Luke could go down some very dark and dangerous paths without a rigorous, custom treatment plan and regular protocols to ensure compliance.

I silenced my inner monologue and tuned back into Dr. McKay's voice just in time for her to stop reading. "That's all of it," she said. I nodded slowly, suggesting that I was taking it all in, but I had heard all I needed to hear minutes earlier.

Lowering her glasses again, Dr. McKay softly spoke. "So, if you don't mind me asking, how do you know Luke's family?"

"Actually, Dr. McKay, I really don't know Luke's family," I replied.

Not entirely understanding what I meant, she leaned forward and said, "So, will his family be taking custody of him at some point?" she asked.

I shook my head and said, "No, they will not. Her dying wish was for him to be left in my custody. She wrote it up, signed it, and sealed it in an envelope addressed to me the night she passed away. Her adopted brother was collecting things from the house and gave me the letter the next day."

Her expression was equal parts sympathetic and perplexed. Perhaps the thought of me having this massive, new responsibility out of the blue had started registering in her brain. Or that it would have been enough on its own without the myriad of psychological disorders Luke potentially suffers from. Or the level of care I would need to provide him. Or the risk he might pose to my own family. Maybe it was all those factors AND the whole Black woman-white kid thing? This was a riddle wrapped in a mystery inside an enigma, and I could tell that even she, with her advanced education and stature, was struggling to reconcile it all.

I thought, "I'd better get used to that look. Seems like I get it every day."

The long drive home from Bedlam gave me time to replay all the details I received from Dr. McKay as Luke slept in the backseat of the car. His diagnosis explained some of the behaviors I'd observed since he'd been staying at my house. Luke hadn't shown any emotion since his mother had died (outside of the fight, but that didn't last long). Undoubtedly, trauma affects different people differently, and kids are no exception to this rule. Like adults, kids can just as masterfully suppress or bottle their emotions inside. But inevitably, all of that bottled-up pain gets expelled. And when it does, it isn't usually in a positive or constructive way.

Luke's behavioral diagnoses were arrived at well before his mother fell ill and long before she passed away. While he may have seemed in a good mood and relatively unfazed by it all, I suspected a clock ticking inside him with something explosive attached. I was committed to him having a safety valve for his emotions. I believed I could leverage my network to find him the right professional. I would need someone to show him how to understand and navigate his feelings while positively reinforcing his compliance with all aspects of the treatment plan.

Given everything I learned about him during our appointment, I was sure he'd need to be reevaluated and put on a new medication regimen. It would be the only way that I could ensure his best interest while protecting the safety and sanctity of our home with him in it.

Looking in my rearview mirror to see the cute youngster sleeping peacefully, I thought, "If I can ensure that he has the resources and support he needs to get through whatever he starts feeling, we might just have a shot."

CHAPTER 22

*T*he next morning, Luke and I had breakfast, and I dropped him off at Justine's house. Among other things, I met with a lawyer that Gio referred me to. The prominent attorney was one of his clients, and while her specialty wasn't family law per se, she still agreed to meet and discuss my situation from a legal standpoint. I knew I'd need something more formal than Dixie's deathbed letter to substantiate my custody of Luke.

I reflected on the previous day while looking for parking in the lot attached to the firm's office building. I thought how fortunate it was that Dr. McKay recognized my name and my work (despite the awkward assumptions she made beforehand). Based on my reputation, she trusted that I would treat Luke's information carefully. Still, I suspected that if I took Luke to see her again (which would never happen because she works at a former asylum called Bedlam), she would be far less willing to share anything without my proof of guardianship. And I wouldn't blame her for that one bit.

I had a seat after entering the firm's offices and signing in with the receptionist. I'd never been through this situation and certainly had no context for what the courts might decide in a haphazard circumstance like this. All I could hope was that it wouldn't be a long, drawn-out process or, worse, one that would prevent us from joining Kinney and the kids as I had planned before all this madness burst into my life. Gio's well-dressed attorney friend had been thoroughly briefed on the situation, thanks to Mr. Melodrama. Our exchange was pleasant, and the conversation made me feel less uncertain. She'd consulted with a colleague in the firm's family law division before my arrival, and they agreed to file a motion for emergency guardianship on my behalf.

She told me what the representation would cost and reminded me of other things I needed to have on my to-do list before the motion was filed. Among them was finding out where Dixie worked, determining whether she had any life insurance policies, and, if so, who the beneficiaries were. There were a few other items on the list that she rattled off, but I was stuck on the first three because I hadn't heard from any of Dixie's family members since that insane funeral, and honestly, I didn't expect to.

After we covered the following steps, I thanked her for her time and effort, exchanged contact information, and returned to the car.

As I left the firm, I thought, "Lawson is the most likely (and level-headed) person to reach out to.

"Hopefully, he can answer a few of these questions for me," I said aloud.

I also planned to speak with the manager at the bank to find out how Charlotte had gotten access to clean out Dixie's bank account.

I'd get right on with all that, but I was just a few minutes away from Tinsley's luxury high-rise. I pinged her, and she was working from home, so I made my way over. I exited the elevator on the 48th floor of her building, which overlooked the north end of downtown Middleton along the riverfront. I always found the view from the elevator lobby breathtaking, but it was just a prelude to the unobstructed views from Tinsley's penthouse-like apartment.

As I neared Tinsley's front door, I could hear her relaxation music playing loudly enough to disturb her neighbors, if she had any. Only three other tenants are on her floor, and by some feat or architectural magic, none of them share a wall. Just outside the door were birds chirping, running water, and melodic sitars playing, which made me laugh. After her last divorce, Tinsley went on a week-long retreat at a remote monastery in some Thai rainforest and returned home as a Buddhist monk. She even built a small stupa of her very own after the divorce was finalized. Her home's artifacts and trinkets represented Buddhist symbolism and traditions – jade, lotus flowers, waterfalls, elephants, and Buddhas.

Tinsley answered the door, wearing her matching workout set and a silk robe. "Hey, love," I said as we greeted each other with a warm embrace.

"I was making a smoothie. Would you like one, hon?" Tinsley asked. "No, I'm good, but thanks."

"Please tell me what's going on with the newest member of your family," she said while giggling and chopping her fruit. Upon her asking, I was hesitant to tell her what I learned from the psychiatrist.

"Well," I said. "I was able to speak to the psychiatrist listed on the pill bottle you found."

"Really?" Tinsley asked in a curious tone.

"Yes, he's been diagnosed with several behavioral disorders, some since he was two years old!"

"Wow...that's why they talk about the kid like he's the devil," Tinsley surmised aloud before turning on the blender.

"Professionally speaking, Naomi, what do you think? Is his

diagnosis something you should be concerned about, especially integrating him with your kids?"

"Well, I'm sure he needs to be on medication, but I plan to have him reevaluated," I replied.

Tinsley shook her head as she started blending her smoothie again. "You know where I stand with the situation," she said, "and my position has not changed. You are my friend, and I care about you. I don't want to see you go through unnecessary problems for doing something good," Tinsley said.

"By problems, what do you mean, Tinsley?"

"Like I was trying to explain to Ferrin that day. I wish all white people could be like me, Naomi. You know, supportive, open-minded, and understanding. Unfortunately, that is not the world we live in."

She continued. "Luke is a white kid, and you are a Black family. People will stare at you guys and whisper…" I cut her off before she could continue.

"Look, Tinsley. I deal with stares and whispers everywhere I go in this community: the grocery store, the department stores, and even the gas station. I'm dressed too nicely, or my car is too nice. You have the gift of anonymity! You walk in, and no one thinks twice about 'why' you are there or whether you belong," I said. "I know all that," Tinsley interrupted. She said, "I mean, I haven't walked a mile in your shoes, but all that will be even worse with a white kid by your side. I mean, people will ask inappropriate questions."

"Inappropriate questions like what?" I snapped. "If Luke, Nick, or Noel were in the bath together, what color would the water turn?" she asked.

There was silence.

"Oh, you are serious?" I said, shocked.

"Tinsley, how foolish is that? I'm very disappointed in you for asking that question. First, why would Luke ever need to be in the bath simultaneously as one of my sons? Secondly, what color would the water turn?" I giggled sarcastically.

"That's my point, Naomi," Tinsley said. "These are the types of questions some people want to know, and we don't want to be judged for asking. I understand these questions may seem offensive to you, but we wonder about these things and don't always have somebody like you to ask," she said apologetically.

"Some ignorant questions do not deserve a response,

Tinsley and I would put that question at the top of the ignorant list."

"Well, have you given some thought if that lowlife man from the funeral wants to fight for custody?"

"No, I said. "I'm just trying to gather as much information as possible about this kid. Gio referred me to a lawyer, and she plans to file a motion for emergency guardianship.

"Naomi," Tinsley said, "I don't want you to be naive about what you are getting yourself into."

"Tinsley, I know you mean well, and yes, this situation is a mess. But I'm trying to do what is best for a kid that has been orphaned."

"I know, honey, and I'm sorry, I didn't mean to upset you," Tinsley said while holding my hand. "I know you and Kinney are great people, and Naomi, you have an enormous heart, but I fear it won't be worth the trouble."

"Maybe you are right, Tinsley. But right now, his mother is dead, and he is too young to fend for himself. He has no one else at this point but me," I shouted.

That was a point she couldn't argue. She gazed into her smoothie as my words sank in, and I looked off into the distance.

I broke our silence.

"The truth is, Luke may very well end up a ward of the state, but I have not gotten that far yet. Remember, this is all new, so I'm crossing things off my list as I go."

She sipped and nodded. I realized I kept talking about Luke and my situation but wanted to change the subject. "Enough about me," I said. "How are you? You and Ferrin were in a weird place the last time I saw you. Have you spoken to her?"

"No," she said. "I have not. We are both passionate individuals, and I'm not sure Ferrin will ever understand the full magnitude of what I was trying to convey.

Naturally, she's an angry person," Tinsley said. "I love Ferrin and spending time with her, but she is angry and can come off a bit radical at times."

Tinsley was still upset with Ferrin and their conversation.

"Tinsley," I said, "I think you both seemed angry. You jumped up and slammed your hands on my table while she stayed seated, so you looked like the aggressor. You all should be able to have those tough conversations, whether you agree or disagree; however, it's important to be mindful of what you say and how you say it."

"I disagree that I was the aggressor," Tinsley said. "I was provoked! She called me a racist, and I don't have one racist bone in my body. You and I would never be friends if I were a racist. She must have forgotten that I've dated Black men before," Tinsley mentioned.

"Tinsley, you know I do not take sides, but I think your communication had an obvious breakdown. Listening is just as important as getting your point across," I said.

"I know," Tinsley interrupted (inadvertently proving my point).

"But she made me so mad. If I'm being honest, I'm still a little pissed off."

I smiled and said, "Oh, you don't say? Well, are you too pissed to be a good host and offer me something besides that thick mess you sipping on?"

"Eww wee, Nay...This smoothie is bad. Let me pour us something a little 'healthier.'"

We visited for another hour before I left to pick up Luke from Justine's house.

* * *

THE EVENING WAS UPON US, and Luke and I were streaming a superhero movie on TV in the family room. I was writing down my checklist of things I needed to do before we could depart for Belize. I figured he'd love it there – being with kids and exploring Dad's property from the fields to the shoreline. It would also give me a preview of how well the kids adjust to being around each other. I've been missing Kinney and the kids. I hoped to have time to myself before reuniting with the family, but the universe had other plans.

Luke seemed excited about going. He said he had never been to a beach before but loved swimming. Luke mentioned his mother used to take him swimming when he was younger. That was the first time I heard him reference his mother, and it was refreshing to hear him mention her. It's been one of my biggest concerns that he hadn't talked about her nor shown any emotion.

"Luke, is that your favorite memory of your mother?" I asked him.

"Yes," he said.

"If you feel sad or want to talk about your mom, I'm here, okay?"

"Okay, but I'm not sad," he replied.

As we were talking, my phone lit up. It was a text from Charlotte asking if I could call her. I sat there looking at my phone and wondered what she wanted to talk to me about. "Maybe she wants Luke after all or knows someone in the family who plans to take him. I guess I can hear her out. I have a few questions about Dixie that she might be able to answer." Understandably, I had zero interest in going to her home and zero interest in her coming to mine. I suggested we meet at a restaurant the next day and thought warming up the relationship could be good for Luke. Although Charlotte is a questionable family member, she may know someone else who is willing to take care of Luke. I'm open to a conversation; however, I will do what I think is best for Luke because I refuse to put him in an unhealthy environment.

I arrived at the restaurant early to choose a table that would give Charlotte and me some privacy. Charlotte arrived at the table, smiling.

"Hello," she said. She seemed more human today than in my last few encounters with her.

"Would you like to order some wine, Charlotte?" I asked. "No, I don't usually drink," she said.

I definitely need this drink while dealing with her. "I was surprised to hear from you, Charlotte. What would you like to talk to me about?"

"I think we should get to know each other better after everything that has happened," she said, looking at me with a slight smile. I almost asked her why, but I just sat silently and let her continue.

"So, how is Luke doing?"

"He seems to be holding up pretty well despite everything," I said as I took a drink of my chardonnay. "Charlotte, I want to address one of the elephants in the room. Why are none of you guys willing to care for Luke? I don't understand how your family can let a stranger raise him?" I said, with a questionable tone.

"I get it," Charlotte said. "It seems mean, and I cannot speak for anyone else in the family, but I can't take him," she said.

"Why, Charlotte?"

"My husband won't allow it, and we have a son. We used to let the two of them play together, but Luke would do things to hurt him.

"What do you mean, hurt him? Were they roughhousing?" I asked.

"Once, he pushed him off the top of the bunk bed, causing my son to sprain his arm," Charlotte said. "Another time, he punched my son in the face and gave him a bloody nose. Luke always did something to him, so we stopped letting him come over."

I'm not sure I believe Charlotte's version of the story because if her son is anything like her, Luke might have been defending himself. Dixie told me Charlotte's daughter slapped her in the face, so it's obvious this family communicates through violence. Let us not forget Charlotte's latest WWE performance with Cash at the funeral.

"So, you won't care for him because the two boys don't get along?" I asked.

"Well, that's not all of it," Charlotte said.

"Then what is it, Charlotte?"

"Luke is evil," she said. "He creeps me out. The way he stares at me gives me chills, and he's very rebellious. My poor mother lived in the house with my sister and him," she said. "If they were not living in the house with her, she might be alive today."

I paused, and my face couldn't hide what was on my mind.

"Was she sitting here implying that Luke or Dixie killed their mom?!"

Aloud, I asked, "What did you mean by 'might be alive,' Charlotte?"

Charlotte answered, "She was always worrying about them. My sister would run off for days, sometimes weeks, leaving my sick mother to look after Luke. He'd scream at my mom and throw stuff around the house when upset. My mom could barely walk, and Luke would take advantage of her. She'd tell him he couldn't leave, and he'd leave anyway, knowing she couldn't physically stop him..."

"Damn, this kid is something else," I thought as Charlotte continued.

"My mom would call my brother over occasionally because she was afraid of what Luke might do to her!"

"He is a small child, but given that she was elderly... with limited mobility... I could see how she *might* have been (afraid of him)," I offered gently.

"That's not the half of it," Charlotte said before pausing. She needed a moment. I suppose the thought of other things he had done was too traumatic or unbelievable for her to share. None of this diminished my skepticism or disdain for her, mind you. But the story she was telling didn't seem fabricated.

Then, out of the blue, she asked, "How did my sister come to know you anyway?"

I paused to consider where she was coming from before I answered. We didn't reside in the same neighborhood (or tax bracket). We didn't belong to the same professional associations or social clubs; our children weren't classmates. Let's face it: if our boys hadn't played together at the park and come over occasionally, we wouldn't know of Luke, Dixie, or any of them.

I replied, "That's the thing, Charlotte...she didn't know me. We had only recently met." I thought, "If she isn't going to help me with Luke, then hopefully she has more helpful information, or this conversation is over."

"Charlotte," I said, "did Dixie have an insurance policy through her job or anywhere?"

"I think she started a new job a couple of months ago," Charlotte said as she bent down, grabbed an envelope, and handed it to me.

"What is this?" I asked.

"Her pay stubs, Luke's birth certificate, Social Security card, and I believe his medical card are in there. These are just a few things I gathered from her house," Charlotte said.

I was surprised she hadn't thrown them in the trash with the rest of Luke's belongings.

"Charlotte, I'm under the impression that you and Dixie were not close. She told me that someone had taken money from her bank account. Do you know anything about that?" I asked. "Whatever she has, or had, belongs to her next of kin unless there is a will that states otherwise."

Charlotte started looking uncomfortable and didn't respond. "Do you know anything about that, Charlotte?" I repeated.

"I was the executor of her estate," she said.

"That's interesting, Charlotte. She told me she did not have one," I said. Although that wasn't true, I was baiting Charlotte to find out whatever I could about this money situation.

Dixie told me that Charlotte stole her money and closed her bank account while in the hospital. Unbeknownst to Charlotte, I was trying to find out if I needed to sue Charlotte and the bank on Luke's behalf.

"So, you appointed yourself the executor over her bank account, not her son...I'm trying to confirm this part because I've hired an attorney. Any information you have regarding her finances would be helpful."

I stared at her to tell her I was serious about this situation. Charlotte quickly stated, "I left you a check for a thousand dollars in that envelope...to help with Luke," she said.

"Is that from Dixie's account?" I asked.

Charlotte's face started to turn red, and she was very uncomfortable but never answered the question. That check was all the proof I needed."Well, I need to get going. Thank you for your time today. Is there anything else before we part ways?" I asked.

She returned the pleasantries with nods and a half-baked smile before softly responding, "Not that I can think of."

"Well, I will be in touch, or my attorney will." I stood up, but

Charlotte was still sitting down. "If you think of anything else," I said, "please give me a call." I wonder if Charlotte met with me to see if she could get away with stealing the money Dixie told me about. I plan to have everything investigated because this family is shady and cannot be trusted.

CHAPTER 23

*T*he big day had finally arrived. In a matter of hours, Luke and I would be on our way to Belize. Luke usually struggled to wake up in the mornings, but on this particular day, he popped right up. We packed last night to avoid being late to the airport. Gio, Ferrin, and Tinsley each had codes for the house so they could come by and check on things whenever needed. I was so excited to reunite with Kinney and the kids. It had only been a few days since they left, but it seemed we had been apart much longer. I was looking forward to six weeks of relaxation on the beach. And it would be the perfect way to put all of this mess with Luke's family aside, at least for a while.

Luke and I made it to the airport and through security well ahead of time. It was his first time traveling via airplane, so the airport fascinated him. I had to keep a firm grip on his hand so he wouldn't take off before the plane! We picked up a few items from different stores on our way to our gate. As usual, I noticed people staring at Luke and me excessively. I almost asked one older man if I could 'help' him because he was staring at us so intensely.

Before the boarding process began, Luke and I printed boarding passes at a nearby kiosk. I handed Luke his pass so he could scan it and board the plane like a big boy. Some of the people seated nearby watched us, including the gate agent who would be inviting us aboard the plane shortly.

A woman's voice came over the airport PA system. "Good morning, ladies and gentlemen. This is a pre-boarding announcement for flight 6155 to Belize City. We are now inviting passengers with small children and any passengers requiring special assistance to begin boarding at this time."

"That's our cue, Luke. You ready?" He nodded vigorously, put his backpack on, and looked at his boarding pass to ensure it was ready to swipe. We stood to the side of the boarding line and allowed five or six elderly and differently-abled passengers to board before us. "They'll need more time than we will, so we'll let them go ahead," I discreetly explained. After a few moments, it was our turn, and Luke was ready. He had watched the people ahead of us go through the process and felt he knew exactly what to do.

We approached the boarding door together, and I motioned Luke ahead of me. I gave the gate agent a polite smile and head nod. She didn't reciprocate. Instead, she looked down at Luke and asked, "Are you flying alone?"

Luke turned and looked at me as if he didn't understand the question. That made two of us...

"You didn't just see me print and hand him his boarding pass right in front of you?!?" I asked both sarcastically and rhetorically.

"Oh! Are you two traveling *together*?" she asked with feigned surprise.

I rolled my eyes dramatically and answered her, "You knew he was with me before we got up here." I turned back to Luke, who had an irritated expression matching mine. "Go ahead and swipe your pass right there," I pointed. He did so, and the agent saw him seated in first class. "Oh, surprised again?" I asked with indignation. I swiped my boarding pass and said, "You know, you could have asked him if this was his first time flying and offered him some wings or something. Instead, you tried to ruin this moment for both of us. Thanks."

I walked off, ignoring her as she apologized. She needed to be 'checked up,' and Luke needed to see me handle it the way I did for context. But, "...ruin our trip before it even began? Not a chance," I thought. We were headed to a tropical paradise for six whole weeks!

The rude exchange with the gate agent gave the slower passengers in front of us all the time they needed to make it down the jetway and into the plane. As we approached the airplane's door, Luke examined the near-empty tunnel with amazement. The baggage handler noticed his awe. The young man waved at me and offered the wide-eyed, first-time flyer a congratulatory fist bump.

"Have a great flight, little man!"

"Thanks, dude!" Luke responded. The handler laughed as I shook my head. I flashed him a nod of gratitude.

We boarded, and to my surprise, no flight attendant was standing there to greet us. I steered Luke toward our seats in the third or fourth row of the plane. Both flight attendants were assisting another passenger toward the middle of the aircraft. As I got our bags in the overhead bin, an older lady stood upright, partially blocking access to our assigned seats.

I looked at my boarding pass and said, "Excuse us, we're in Seats 4A and 4B. Did they give you 4B, too?"

She looked me up and down before asking Luke, "Honey, are you okay?" Her gaze was piercing as she waited for him to answer. Luke huffed and moved past her into the window seat. "Nicely done," I thought.

Sensing the woman's 'to catch a predator' vibe, I steeled myself for another unwelcome and unwarranted exchange.

"The devil is just going to keep testing me today…" I said to myself. I motioned toward my assigned seat next to Luke. The woman moved to block me from my seat entirely and was now physically separating me from the boy.

"I think it would be best to exchange seats," the woman said.

I recall my eyes fluttering with disbelief. "You need to move out of my way and out of my seat right now, ma'am."

"No, I don't," she said, with a defiant tone and look.

"Mind your own business, and GO TO YOUR SEAT, ma'am!" I raised my voice loud enough to attract the flight attendants' attention in the middle of the cabin. By this point, other status passengers were entering the plane. Many were in the gate area and witnessed my first troublesome exchange. I thought, "Here we go again. Us at the center of an issue neither of us invited or provoked."

"Is everything okay here?" the female flight attendant asked.

"No. We're not okay at all." I replied.

The older woman was obviously a master storyteller. "I was just standing here, and this little boy got on the plane by himself. I just didn't want him flying alone. Not with a stranger, so I offered to switch seats with her. Then, she got mad and started yelling at me."

"That's not what happened! He and I are together! We are in seats 4A and B. I went to sit, and she physically blocked me from sitting with my boy."

That one took them by complete surprise. They looked at him and looked at me in an attempt to make it make sense. The male flight attendant stood in the row of first-class seats just behind ours and asked Luke, "What about you, little guy? Are you okay?"

"Is he okay?!? Why wouldn't he be? Is it your policy to ask every child on every flight if they're okay, or just *this* child? He'll be fine once she MOVES out of my seat!"

From the window, a confused and exasperated Luke muttered, "I just want to sit with my momma, Naomi, please."

I held up my boarding pass. "Naomi Martinez. Platinum 10K. 4B." The female flight attendant motioned the older woman to move out of my way.

The misguided Karen was crushed with shame and embarrassment. "Well, I just thought that he was…"

"Don't bother. We all *know* what you thought." I said.

I took my seat and noticed her bag under the seat in front of me. I placed it in the aisle. The male flight attendant grabbed it and asked the humiliated over-stepper, "Ma'am, let's see your boarding pass and get you to your assigned seat. 14…B?!?"

All of the passengers in earshot moaned and began complaining audibly. "You gotta be fucking kidding me, said one first-class passenger as he waited impatiently to sit down. Another, waiting for the fiasco to end, said, "I can't believe this… the nerve."

At this point, I was sitting there, shaking my head in disbelief. It felt like everyone on the plane saw or heard what had just transpired, so why was I the one feeling ashamed and embarrassed?

The male flight attendant returned and said, "Ma'am, I just wanted to ensure you and the child are okay."

"Well, it's pretty obvious that we aren't," I replied flatly. "That woman believed her racist assumption about us so much that she physically separated us from one another, and neither of you were here to prevent it. All of these passengers were held up in the jetway as a result. And now you're asking whether or not I'm okay?!?"

"Okay, calm down," the male flight attendant ordered.

"Calm down?! I was trying to before you approached me. Please, go on. I'll deal with customer service and have this reported before we hit 10,000 feet." I pulled our tablets and earphones out of my tote bag and shooed him away.

The female flight attendant came down from the cockpit area and instructed the male flight attendant to resume his duties in the back of the plane. She knelt beside my seat and said, "I'm sorry that happened to you. I should have been up here, but that one can't do anything on his own. I'll take good care of you two and ensure the airline shows special appreciation for your continued loyalty. Now, what can I bring you to drink?"

"One of everything, please."

We laughed, as did a few other passengers within earshot of her apology. I turned to see Luke's face pressed against the glass, watching all the activities taking place outside the plane. "Oh, that's my suitcase on that belt thing! Yours too, Naomi. They'll be under us in the sky, huh?"

"Yes, they sure will," I smiled.

We got comfortable in our seats, powered up our devices, and put my noise-canceling headphones around my neck. I replayed the last several minutes of the boarding process and tried not to get angry again. The look of failure and humiliation on Karen's face helped more than she'd ever know.

"I'll be expecting at least two round-trip tickets for this one!" I thought to myself. "This was exactly the mess Tinsley was talking about," I bristled. After all, she had warned me over and over again. As the plane started to move, I focused my attention on Luke, who was bouncing in his seat. His gamut of emotions (wonder, excitement, and nervousness) were incredibly cute to watch. It was a pleasant reprieve from the chaos we'd just endured.

As we gathered speed and began to leave the ground, I saw and appreciated what anyone would have observed: a harmless little boy, innocently and fully immersed in the biggest thrill of his young life, a thrill that I was making possible.

* * *

I PLACED my headphones over my ears and stretched out a bit. It was a chance for me to decompress for the first time in over a week. I couldn't resist asking myself, "What if this situation had been the other way around? If I was a white woman, and Luke was a black kid, would these strangers have the same concerns? Probably not. In fact, they'd probably breathe a sigh of relief and feel *better* about his welfare."

I let that sink in for a moment.

"Time and time again, I'd seen human interest, 'feel-good' stories of affluent white families adopting melanated children from here (and abroad). They were put on public stages to be celebrated. They were recognized as great humans. Rewarded with houses, cars, financial support, and more. One of their stories was so powerful and soul-stirring that they made a movie about it that won an award."

I glanced over at Luke. He was resting comfortably, enjoying his tablet and a juice box specially delivered by the female flight attendant. What if this flight had gone the other way around? If any of these people knew the week I'd just had, they'd be rolling out a red carpet for us. If that woman knew what brought Luke and me together, she would have given me a standing ovation rather than a standing order to find another seat. How much better would I feel at this very moment? How much better would he feel? What kind of hope would we inspire if people knew about our relationship? Or if they'd assume the best instead of the worst? You get a car. You get a car. Naomi, You get a car!" I jokingly replied to myself.

My dubious inner voice didn't waste a moment kicking in.

"Naomi, when have Black women *ever* been praised for raising white children? We've been raising white babies since the 'Old South,' and that was at the expense of our own children and families. It was a sign of wealth, power, and privilege then, and the same thing is true today."

But here I was. Highly educated and titled, professional and refined. When confronted with an impossible situation that nothing could have prepared me for, I didn't retreat or surrender. I stepped up. But for no other reason than my skin, I'd been met with doubt and skepticism at least once every time we were together in public.

"Maybe I should make a shirt that says, 'No, he's not in danger. No, I'm not the help'!"

That was the last thought I had on the subject before winding my neck, tilting my head, and closing my eyes. I wasn't sure what my journey with Luke had in store beyond a well-deserved tropical getaway for the next several weeks. That would be enough for the moment.

"Sure, Kinney and I will have quite a bit to sort through when we return, but we'll be fine. We're always fine." Or, so I thought, until we landed.

—THE END—

ABOUT THE AUTHOR

NOON WESTBROOK

Noon Westbrook shares the experiences that have defined, inspired, and influenced her life in narrative form.

She is always in storyteller mode, traveling the world and interacting with everyday people as an anthropologist. Noon has never met a stranger, and through observation, inquiry and listening, she assembles and weaves stories that distinguish, relay and connect our collective, human experiences.

Noon, who holds degrees in Liberal Arts (B.A.), Sociology (B.A.) and Higher Education Administration (M.A.) began her writing journey during a sabbatical from pursuing her Ph.D. in Education.

In a recent interview, she explained, "For years, I ignored my family. I ignored my friends. I ignored them telling me over and over to write my story. I happened upon a Maya Angelou quote that read, "There is no greater agony than bearing an untold story inside you." Their encouragement and a legend's choice words moved me to finally do it. And this story is only the beginning."

From family drama to mystery and horror, Noon's narrative explorations are inspired by real people and events, grounding every tale she weaves in reality — captivating readers of all types along the way.